Paris Metro Tales

PARIS METRO TALES

Stories translated by

Helen Constantine

OXFORD
UNIVERSITY PRESS

OXFORD
UNIVERSITY PRESS

Great Clarendon Street, Oxford OX2 6DP

Oxford University Press is a department of the University of Oxford.
It furthers the University's objective of excellence in research, scholarship,
and education by publishing worldwide in

Oxford New York

Auckland Cape Town Dar es Salaam Hong Kong Karachi
Kuala Lumpur Madrid Melbourne Mexico City Nairobi
New Delhi Shanghai Taipei Toronto

With offices in

Argentina Austria Brazil Chile Czech Republic France Greece
Guatemala Hungary Italy Japan Poland Portugal Singapore
South Korea Switzerland Thailand Turkey Ukraine Vietnam

Oxford is a registered trade mark of Oxford University Press
in the UK and in certain other countries

Published in the United States
by Oxford University Press Inc., New York

British Library Cataloguing in Publication Data
Data available

Library of Congress Cataloging in Publication Data
Library of Congress Control Number: 2010940320

Typeset by SPI Publisher Services, Pondicherry, India
Printed in Great Britain
on acid-free paper by
Clays Ltd, St Ives plc

ISBN 978-0-19-957980-8

1 3 5 7 9 10 8 6 4 2

Contents

Picture Acknowledgements   ix

Introduction   1

Gare du Nord ⬚1   13
Jacques Réda

Saint-Julien-le-Pauvre ⬚2   19
Julien Green

Summer Rain ⬚3   27
Marie Desplechin

Refined ⬚4   49
Daniel Boulanger

A Little Accident ⬚5   55
Colette

If it were Sunday ⬚6   61
Annie Saumont

Facino Cane 7   77
Honoré de Balzac

Rue des Larmes 8   101
Frédéric Fajardie

Story 9   119
Paul Fournel

There or Elsewhere 10   139
Martine Delerm

Saint Genevieve 11   143
Jacques de Voragine

Expomodigliani.com 12   157
Martine Delerm

Minuet 13   163
Guy de Maupassant

Snow 14   173
Émile Zola

La Halle 15   183
Gérard de Nerval

Confronting the Present 16   197
Andrée Chedid

The Cab 17   207
Théodore de Banville

The Little Restaurant at Ternes 18   217
Georges Simenon

Romance in the Metro 19   251
Claude Dufresne

The Neighbour in the Rue de Jarente 20   265
Cyrille Fleischman

The Landlady 21   275
Guy de Maupassant

La Butte Montmartre 22   287
Gérard de Nerval

Notes on the Metro   294

Notes on the Stories   303

Notes on the Authors   314

Selected Further Reading   317

Publisher's Acknowledgements   320

Map   324

Picture Acknowledgements

Pages 12, 54, 182: © Roger-Viollet/TopFoto

Pages 18, 60, 76, 100, 138, 142, 162, 172, 216, 250, 264, 274, 286: © Helen Constantine

Page 26: © Alison Stieglitz/iStockphoto

Page 48: © Renaud Visage/Photolibrary.com

Page 118: © FA/Roger-Viollet/TopFoto

Page 156: detail from *Jeanne Hébuterne*, 1919, by Amedeo Modigliani. Private collection. © The Bridgeman Art Library

Page 196: © Anna Gleen/Fotolia

Page 206: detail from *Boulevard Poissonnière in the Rain*, c. 1885, by Jean Béraud. Musée de la Ville de Paris, Musée Carnavalet, Paris. © The Art Gallery Collection/Alamy

Page 318: © Eye-Stock/Alamy

Introduction

Below the City of Light is the immense black hole of the Paris metro. This network of tunnels, built at the turn of the twentieth century, and which held such a fascination for Zazie, Raymond Queneau's famous heroine, is loved by Parisians and visitors alike. Under the occupation of Paris by the Nazis in 1941 it was one of the few places where Jews were tolerated, and was also used extensively by the Resistance during those years. In the cold winter of 1954 the directors of the metro, moved by the words of the young Abbé Pierre who throughout his life did so much for homeless people, made over three stations to the homeless, who still sometimes take refuge in its warmth on icy nights. It currently serves nearly 5 million passengers each day and, with its younger sibling, the RER, provides a speedy and efficient way of getting around the city. It is a manageable and often entertaining means of transport, where in one corridor or another you may hear the sound of a flautist playing Mozart or the maracas of a Peruvian band. It is always a surprise to arrive at Saint-Michel or Denfert-Rochereau or any of the 350 stations and emerge out of the hole into another area of Paris. Entrances to the metros, even those not decorated by the art nouveau artist Hector Guimard, are particularly alluring—the metro entrance at Lamarck-Caulaincourt, for example, which features in the popular film *Amélie*, and is built into the hill of Montmartre. Whatever station it may be, the combination of the steps, trees, cafés, and surrounding buildings as you arrive presents a composite picture that delights the eye and induces a sense of excitement and discovery.

The connection between the metro and this book is the stories you are about to read. Coming up from underground, you leave behind its peculiar smell, which was once described as 'something between burnt air and rotting bananas'. Attempts were made to sanitize it for the centenary of the metro at the turn of this century, but it still retains its characteristic and nostalgic odour. As you reach the fresh air you have a moment's disorientation and try to get your bearings. A brief look at the map on the hoarding by the entrance steps may help. In this neighbourhood—in every neighbourhood—there are many stories, factual and fictional, to be discovered: in a nearby park, on the wall of a church, down a sidestreet, in a café. I hope this book of tales set in Paris may help readers discover some of those stories for themselves. The metro is where you start; though, as always in Paris, there will be a certain amount of foot-slogging for those who enjoy that too. And I have suggested an itinerary for any who like to follow a plan, though no reader is bound to do that. Pick and choose as you like; don't do it all in one day... Indeed, if you don't even visit this city in person, you may still, as an armchair traveller, enjoy these stories and no sore feet involved.

The structure of *Paris Tales* was provided by the twenty arrondissements of Paris, each story corresponding to one of these areas. This collection follows a pattern too, except that now the readers' starting-point is the all-important metro. You are invited to find your way through the underground, changing trains when necessary and coming up to read a particular story where it takes place. So at the station Ternes we emerge to read Simenon's mysterious 'The Little Restaurant at Ternes', and at Opéra we read Colette's account of a traffic accident, which takes place in a street nearby. It is, in effect, a literary tour of Paris by underground. Readers will find notes on each metro station at the back of the book, with a map and directions for taking the correct metro line to the next story's location.

There are also some notes about the stories and their writers and some suggestions for further reading.

If you buy your *carnet* of metro tickets in advance, you won't have to join the queue of travellers trying to do that at the ticket office in the Gare du Nord. This is where our literary journey starts and finishes; however, you don't *have* to start here and you may have more time on the way back to read the piece by Jacques Réda in which he evokes its particularity and incidentally tells us some surprising news about the station itself. There are twenty-two stories, as in the companion volume, *Paris Tales*. Mainly they range in time from the nineteenth to the twenty-first century, but one is translated from the lives of saints collected by Jacques de Voragine in the *Légende dorée* towards the end of the thirteenth century, the story of Saint Genevieve, the patron saint of Paris. Her image is present in many locations, for example in the Luxembourg gardens; carved in the wall of the church of Saint-Étienne du Mont near the Sorbonne; and at the Pont de la Tournelle, where a huge statue of Genevieve by the sculptor Landowski towers above the Seine. Favourite authors reappear—Balzac's 'Facino Cane' is the strange story of a blind musician near the Bastille; Maupassant is represented by 'Minuet', and by 'The Landlady', concerning a law student and his landlady in the Rue des Saints-Pères.

And while Gérard de Nerval evokes an era that is past in his vivid description of the traders in the vast market of Les Halles, much of his itinerary in Montmartre can still be followed. The nineteenth-century writer Théodore de Banville is perhaps not as well known as he should be this side of the Channel, so I have translated a story of his called 'The Cab', about a married couple, which readers may find amusing and perhaps typically Parisian. Of more modern writers, Colette, Georges Simenon, Julien Green will probably be familiar names; Frédéric Fajardie, Martine Delerm, Marie Desplechin, Paul Fournel, Claude Dufresne may not be, but deserve to be better known to anglophone readers.

We see Paris in all seasons, in all weathers: Julien Green advises us to visit the church of Saint-Julien-le-Pauvre, not far from Notre Dame, in the blazing heat of midsummer; Zola shows us how beautiful Paris can be in the snow; and Martine Delerm, in a clever juxtaposition of two stories in 'Expomodigliani.com', shows us how wretched it can be; Maupassant's story 'Minuet' takes place in May in the Luxembourg gardens and Simenon's story, subtitled 'A Christmas Tale for Grown-ups', is set in the Ternes area of the city on Christmas Eve.

The location of some of these stories is actually in the metro itself: Annie Saumont's evocation of the lives of two teenage girls, for example, told with her characteristic flashbacks and breathless stream-of-consciousness style; Claude Dufresne's humorous and poignant account of Hilaire Robichon, whose humdrum life is abruptly turned upside down when a glamorous woman sits in the seat next to him at Bastille station; Andrée Chedid's story of a man experiencing an existential crisis as he makes the long journey across Paris to meet an old flame at the Porte de Clignancourt. But to discover some of these stories, not least because some were written before the metro was built in 1898–9, you must leave the metro behind you and explore the world above ground.

Short stories come in all shapes and sizes. That will be evident from this collection, which includes a variety of humorous, tragic, historical, sociological, and ludic stories representative of much short French fiction. One Oulipian text, which I was unable in the end to include, was Georges Perec's 'Tentative d'épuisement d'un lieu parisien' ('An attempt at an exhaustive description of a place in Paris'), in which he tries to note everything that happens in the Place Saint Sulpice within a certain time and space. But Paul Fournel's story, whose French title is 'Roman' (novel), is also Oulipian. Like Perec, Fournel belongs to that group of writers in the tradition of Raymond Queneau for whom playing with language and literary forms is an important ingredient of their work. His 'roman' is told in seven different ways and from seven different perspectives—Fournel identifies with each of his characters, adding other, satirical dimensions to the basic plot. The story may call to mind *Exercices de style*, by Oulipo's founder, Queneau, in which ninety-nine different stylistic devices are used to recount the same story. I admit I was hard-pressed to find a valid metro location for Paul Fournel's story; in the end I settled on Glacière, the nearest station to the grim Prison de la Santé where the man in Fournel's story is visited by the mother and her little boy. Another brand of humour, this time blackly funny, is provided by Daniel Boulanger in his story set in Père Lachaise cemetery, in the east of Paris, and again we see the characteristic playing with language, so integral a component of much modern French prose, as parallels are drawn between the aunt's cremation and the dinner enjoyed by her nephew.

The short story as a literary form has its devotees and has risen in popularity recently, with more festivals and competitions dedicated to promoting it, and a consequently greater appreciation of the constraints and opportunities it presents. Writers of short stories have to extend and develop, add another dimension to what perhaps began life as an image, a brief encounter, or even just a feeling. The success or failure of a story—its haunting quality, whether it lingers in the mind—may depend upon this expansion. One technique a writer may use is that of juxtaposing different times and places: alongside or behind the first narrative runs a second, as in the story by Martine Delerm about Jeanne Hébuterne, mistress of Modigliani. The common factor here is the exhibition of Modigliani paintings in the Musée du Luxembourg. To add another dimension to her story, Annie Saumont uses flashback so that we understand her characters in terms of their childhood and background; to achieve a similar depth of character Fajardie deliberately confuses the chronology of his story, placing his hero in a sort of limbo as he hovers between the violent events of 1968 and 1973, not knowing in his mental anguish as he wanders the Rue de Lappe which decade he is living in; Marie Desplechin attempts to analyse and convey two different states of mind in her story, set in République and Belleville, about a depressive. Balzac's tale of the adventurer, 'Facino Cane', while set very firmly in the contemporary atmosphere of his twelfth arrondissement of Paris in the Rue de Charenton, evokes and contrasts with that the former adventurous life of his hero in Venice.

Length is another consideration. More than the novel, the short story must condense and suggest, and is perhaps in this respect more akin to a poem. There is no room for extraneous information; it all must belong together, with each part a meaningful piece of the jigsaw. Impossible to prescribe an ideal length, for every story will set its own limitations and parameters. So in this volume short pieces like Martine Delerm's sit alongside longer stories like Balzac's. I have aimed at variety in this respect as well as in tone and style. But none of these tales is overly long and each can be read at a sitting, on a park bench, in a café, or in an armchair.

When is a story not a story, but a 'short fiction' or 'text'? Some of the pieces I have chosen might not be considered 'real stories' by some readers: those by Nerval, Réda, or Zola, for instance. I have included them nevertheless for the same reason that I included similar things in my previous volume—because they are in themselves inspired pieces of writing which strongly evoke the sense of place and because they contain within them many stories or shreds of lives which will touch and intrigue the reader. The modern reader will in any case appreciate that much writing is a blurring of fact and fiction. Whenever we tell stories, our imagination works on the given facts, and inevitably those 'facts' will be changed in the telling.

Translating is a mixture of craft and compromise. One of the problems is how to transpose as accurately as possible from one language to another and from one culture to another the voice of the original writer, their individual timbres, their peculiar style and tone. Translating a novel, you begin a relationship with its author which grows in knowledge and understanding as you proceed. In this anthology, however, there are almost a score of writers, each with their own signature, so the relationships are many. What I have tried to do is indicate something of each special voice to the reader, though I do not claim to have always succeeded. I hope I have captured enough of each text to give some idea of it and perhaps to inspire my readers to read more of these extraordinary writers, who deserve to be better known in our own language.

I am very grateful to David Constantine for his translations of the two texts by Gérard de Nerval and for his invaluable suggestions; to Paul Fournel of the French Institute and Annie Saumont for sending me their stories as soon as I mentioned this project to them; to Jacques Réda; to Mary-Ann for doing the enjoyable foot-slogging round Paris with me on various occasions; and to Simon, as always, for his technical support. I should also like to thank Jacqueline Baker, Ariane Petit, Deborah Protheroe, Coleen Hatrick, and the enthusiastic team at OUP who have encouraged and advised me whenever I needed them.

This volume, one of a series of City Tales, is dedicated to all who love Paris, including my former sixth-formers at Bartholomew School, Eynsham, with whom I shared some unforgettable school trips.

The Gare du Nord

Jacques Réda

How many times have I got lost trying to get from the Gare de l'Est to the Gare du Nord, stations in such close proximity as the crow flies? And done the same, of course, in the other direction? The reason one is thwarted in this way resides in its topography: at the Chabrol-Magenta crossroads, like where the Rue de Dunkerque leaves you at the Aqueduc-Lafayette junction, it obliges you to make a wide detour outwards, or else get locked into a labyrinth of little streets among which you will perhaps find the Rue des Deux Gares not the least alluring. From this nervous quest the Saint-Quentin market offers an agreeable diversion. It has been restored, and its new glass panes reflect a nickel-plated sky. The interior has been painted in two contrasting tones—a very dark greeny-blue, the colour of roquefort, and salmon pink—yet they unite in joyful harmony, like a small polyphony of trumpets in a tapestry of greyhounds and medieval headdresses. As a result the slim columns on which the structure rests look even slimmer, alternating the colours or combining them in spirals, like lances in a tournament. They exactly match the smells of cheese and fish doing battle with one another. Let's not stay here too long. There's nothing more disconcerting than the disappearance of a station, especially if you need to catch a train. It's as if the point of departure, playing its role to the extreme, had taken itself off without waiting for you or leaving any trace behind. Now the strange idea of a station that has caught the train is in fact the adventure that really happened to the Gare du Nord around the middle of last century, though not of course all at once: stone by stone it went, to Lille where it was reconstructed; the one we admire rose up in its place around 1863.

Along with the Gare de Lyon, the Gare du Nord is the station that corresponds most precisely to the idea of a major terminal, that exists more or less consciously in one's mind. If the station again took it into its head to go travelling and changed its function, wherever it ended up you would still know it was a station or a former station (or even that it was the Gare du Nord), whether in the polar glaciers or the jungles of Yucatan. It's a question of its physical appearance—a very tricky question in fact, in a sphere where railways are distinguished only by their departure from the norm, since they have for many years conformed to architectural models of a period before they appeared. Through them the specific nature of the station asserts itself by a hundred additional characteristics, more or less striking from one station to another. I am put in mind of London pubs, easily reached from the Gare du Nord via Boulogne and Newhaven. In them you come across all sorts of unbelievably different human beings, who nonetheless embody in an incontrovertible fashion the English type. However, only some of them will remain typical when taken out of their surroundings. That's all I am trying to say. Once that's understood, we can, with care, reintroduce the notion of classical and baroque in order to distinguish the Gare du Nord from the Gare de Lyon. The former, at least in its façade, which runs for 160 metres along the Rue de Dunkerque, brings Greece to life in the spirit of Germany just prior to Nietzsche. It displays an abundance of statues in robes, with crowns, the cities of its network, each with a sort of shield of Athene bearing its coat of arms. If you count them you will find there are twenty-three. Paris reigns, quite as one would expect, at the top, having on her right, one level below, Brussels and Warsaw, then (still lower down, where the pediment finishes) Amsterdam and Frankfurt. Symmetrically to her left are London, Vienna, Berlin, and Cologne, in that order, forming in their entirety a small European congress ruled by a subtle etiquette, which may be explained by political history and doesn't offend anyone's feelings. The other fourteen statues symbolize French towns, from right to left—always in relation to Paris—Boulogne, Compiègne, Douai, and Dunkerque, two by two on each of the two buildings at the side, and in the middle (flanking the clock and the date of completion: 1864) Saint-Quentin, Cambrai, Calais, and Valenciennes. Finally, underneath this last group: Beauvais, Lille, Amiens, Rouen, Arras, and Laon. The principles determining this distribution remain impenetrable. They have ceased to be arbitrary—if indeed they ever were—in that they demonstrate the union of harmony and chance. But behind this rather majestic façade, which manages to sublimate it, the world of the railway overwhelms you in all its harshness. And in that respect as well the Gare du Nord achieves archetypal status. There is always something banging, something draughty and unswept, that makes the first hall seem insane. And then

the ticket-machines!—From which, for a small obla-
tion, of the many called to Sunday at La Courneuve a
few are chosen and receive their return tickets. As for
the arrival and departure halls giving on to the tracks,
the space seems to be permanently cluttered. A wooden
structure, half-club, half-sacristy, takes up the back wall,
trying to introduce a note of orderliness and cosiness
which the new platforms don't even attempt—they are
served by an icy system of escalators underground. You
pass from the old universe of the traveller into the silent
flow of the almost abstract modern world; while upstairs, under the glass roof, the great burning steel monsters with the high wheels and the long oily rods chunter
rhythmically, the porters in smocks with brass badges
shout and farewells are said. Like the untiring waves of
the sea towards which it is heading, all this ceaseless to-
ing and fro-ing continues to burden and cast a gloom
over the Gare du Nord. Perhaps because it has itself been
separated from its first memories, the wind of separa-
tion blows through it permanently. From La Chapelle
the overground metro affords a terrifying view of the
exit, where, like surgeon's knives in a wide-open black
bag, the rails shine at night under the ghostly glow of the
Sacré-Coeur, under the last splashes of the long porno-
graphic meat-factory that gapes near Barbès. The
Goutte d'Or up above is in darkness.

Saint-Julien-Le-Pauvre

Julien Green

It's in the blazing heat of midsummer that one should push open the rather rickety door on those treasures of coolness. I go in and stand quite still. Only the faintest murmur of the great voice of Paris reaches here, and it is hushed by the greater silence in this little church. The solid pillars are all rose-pink in the afternoon sun filtering through the narrow, clear glass windows with their surround of blue tiles. They hold aloft the Romanesque vault, while below them thoughts wing their way like birds between branches in a wood; they are so strong, so still, you'd think they are awaiting the Last Judgement, in a contemplation that sets them apart from the century, and, like kings absorbed in their dreams of splendour, they rise above that modern *weltschmerz* which afflicts my own being too, and, all unawares, bestow upon me a little of that peace which they hold within themselves. Their heads, crowned with foliage, are borne before the altar like caskets of offerings in a procession that has lasted for eight centuries; here a winged siren, there a Christian knight, the symbols of profound ideas progressing forth under the rounded heavens of their vaults.

In this place, perhaps, Dante knelt, between these green walls that look as though an ocean has left behind trails of seaweed. In this place the visionary spoke to the Unseen Presence and later recalled a small street in Paris where he rested awhile in meditation on his journey to the utmost depths of the inner world.

It is very hard nowadays to imagine the sumptuous past of Saint-Julien-Le-Pauvre, which seems to have been waiting for the sadness of our modern age to fully deserve its epithet. We can only with difficulty imagine this church at a time when a priory stood next door and fifty monks chanted beneath its arches, and it is a little hard to comprehend that one of the most beautiful ceremonies of the Middle Ages took place in this building which our spiritual poverty has rendered so humble. Yet it was here that the Sorbonne's *rector magnificus* passed to his successor the ermine gown and velvet sack bag containing the seal of the university. And it was here too that on 11 June every year the whole community of the university assembled in great pomp to proceed thence to the *lendit* fair, where they bought the parchment they needed. At dawn, the Rue Galande, the Rue du Fouarre, the Rue Saint-Séverin, and the Rue Saint-Jacques were roused by the drums and trumpets of the scholars, many carrying lances, swords, or sticks for no other reason than that they were young and had a natural liking for loud noises. What remains, except the name, of all the lively, noisy, joyous animation in this *quartier*, the life of an age that we cannot equal? The life of the Rue du Fouarre, which name reminds me that Pope Urban V enjoined the students not to sit on benches, but at the very feet of their master. Now sitting on the ground is hard, and the boys ran to the sellers of *feurre*, or straw, who sold their wares in the shadow of Saint-Julien. We must suppose that Dante, like everyone else, went off to get his bale of straw right there, to go and hear the lessons of his good master Brunetto Latini, whom he later swiftly consigned to hell, getting his own back as it were, by slipping the name of the little Rue du Fouarre into a tercet about Paradise.

The seventeenth century shook its ignorant wig at the venerable church and pronounced it barbaric. No doubt they thought it too insignificant to completely modernize. And no doubt Saint-Julien, which was at the very end of the Romanesque period but already deferring to the first stirrings of the new style, did not have, in the opinion of Mansart's contemporaries, that Gothic appearance which they found so irritating and attempted to eradicate altogether in the choir-stalls of Saint-Séverin, the more unfortunate neighbour of Saint-Julien-Le-Pauvre. But it was the prior of Saint-Julien himself who shortened the nave and Romanesque door with a façade the tonsured fool imagined was Doric. In our own time, the final metamorphosis: a wide iconostasis installed by popes from the east cleft in two what remained of one of the most beautiful and ancient churches in Paris.

Such as it is, however, the church has still conserved its graceful strength and mysterious youthfulness. One can imagine it in the midst of the fields, for it has the charm of a country church. Its solid, simple aspect is a long way from the feverish thrusts of Saint-Séverin, which bends in upon itself and is decorated with great ragged patches of shade. Saint-Julien welcomes the daylight and retains the light between its walls until dusk. It is solid, firm, and composed like the arguments of Saint Thomas. Neither doubt nor anguished visions will ever come to disturb its serene and thoughtful solitude. A monk with a simple heart, it sits in a white robe beside the river of Gaul.

In the old days, when you pushed open the little side door inside the church, you would find yourself in a delightful little patch of wilderness where you stepped through tall grass among some of the most ancient stones in Paris. Next to the chevet of Saint-Julien one of the last pieces of the Philip Augustus wall, so-called, jutted up from among the grasses like a rock sticking up out of the sea; and a tree, still leafy and waving in the breeze, died slowly beneath the weight of several centuries. Who remembers this place now, so conducive to reverie? In the distance the towers of Notre-Dame, that look white in the storm, appeared black against the July sky, and from time to time a tugboat on the Seine gave a long melancholic call, its hazy note lingering and vanishing into the blue depths. But the sounds of Paris seemed to fade away at the borders of this little place of solitude where I loved to meditate. The silence around me was like a dwelling in which the past had taken refuge; it seemed to me that the whole of Romanesque France inhabited this inner peace and that the ancient stones of Saint-Julien were its visible image. That was what attracted me, round about my sixteenth year. I came across the small church in the course of my wanderings; I have been back many times since.

It sometimes happens that we do things without realizing, and their meaning only becomes clear to us very much later, yet they seem to be dictated by the most watchful part of ourselves. In the spring of 1940, which ended so disastrously for civilized Europe, I instinctively went to those places in Paris which held the most memories, and spent a long time in certain churches which I had not expected would be lost to me so soon. Saint-Julien was the one I found it most difficult to leave: once I had crossed the threshold to go out, I crossed it again a moment later, seized by an anxiety too vague to be expressed in words, and cast one final look on those pillars upon which the setting sun was shedding its last melancholic rays.

Summer Rain

Marie Desplechin

I've done something stupid with Hervé. Last night as
we were leaving the restaurant, I asked him:

'Are you in a car?'

'Yes, shall I take you to the taxi rank?'

'Would you like me to stay tonight?' I said.

That was my mistake. He bent his head. I knew what
he was thinking: maybe I'll stop, look at her, then kiss
her full on her lips, or rather on her cheek, or I'll put
my hand on her neck, or say something, anything, it's
idiotic, I'm an idiot. Tough, I haven't said anything.
And here's my car.

But when he opened the car door, I caught hold of
his shoulder, kissed him full on the lips, then on the
cheek, and I put my hand on his neck.

'I'm an idiot,' I said.

'No, no, you're not. I mean, you're not in the least idiotic.'

He was mumbling. He started the car.

We went to his place. It's so odd making love to someone who's been your friend for so many years. Despite our laughing and joking, I had the feeling all night I was betraying a good friend. Too much companionship, not enough passion. When he fell asleep, I lay in the dark without moving, my eyes open, thinking quietly to myself. Thoughts fluttered through my head like birds in a cage, sometimes hitting the sides. I didn't really know why I'd had the idea of sleeping with him. Unless it was because he had wanted to for so long.

In the morning I struggled into consciousness. A fierce sun beat through the curtainless window. Hervé was asleep on his front. Slowly I turned my head. Very gently I pushed back the covers. I put one foot on the floor, then the other, and got out of bed.

On the tiles in the bathroom, half-eaten away by the water, was a piece of flaky soap. I hurriedly washed and rinsed in cold water. Sometimes my thoughts are so clear they hurt my eyes. All I could find to dry myself was one towel, a small white threadbare towel.

I went into the kitchen. The window over the sink looked out on to a paved yard. An acacia tree leaned awkwardly in the corner. Under the acacia someone was mending his scooter.

Seven o'clock. I drank a Nescafé, sitting at the tiled table. Then I lit a cigarette. Contentment and fatigue took over, and made their way from my heart up to my brain. The morning cigarette always reminds me of other mornings, in a car, a sleeping town, on a country road. I should have dearly liked to go to sleep there and then, serene, among layers of memory.

The door shut softly behind me. Outside it was bright daylight. I only had to go out of the door to enjoy the sunshine, buy the paper, and have breakfast. To be free and at peace. I looked at the closed door.

We must always finish what we start. If we go into an apartment we have to come out. If we sign a contract for a job we have to put in the hours. If we are born we must die. I wondered if Hervé was about to come out on to the landing, take my arm, and carry me back to bed so that I would go to sleep again. I should have liked to be looked after. But I didn't want to go back to bed with Hervé. Not this morning, anyway. I often wonder if the broken bits will, by some miracle, put themselves together again and rebuild what's been destroyed. I turned my back on the door. I pulled my bag up on my shoulder and pressed the lift button.

A few minutes later, I was crossing the Place de la République, in the special peace of morning. The green cleaning-lorries were jolting their way along the pavements and sprinkling them at random with their jets. A hundred metres from the square there was a café on the corner at the beginning of the Rue du Temple. The *patronne* was mopping the tiled floor. I strode across the room. I threw my bag down on the seat and sat down at my table, a small one near the window.

In the sun, with bread and a bowl of tea in front of me, I felt good. I was on my own and my pockets were full of coins. Happiness was within my grasp. It was a lovely warm, soft feeling, airy and light as a brioche.

Then it happened, all at once, quite markedly and without any warning. My world began to disintegrate. Time, inflexible, stretched out before me. The breathing in my chest became more rapid. The ghost of happiness imploded in my head. My feeling of plenitude turned upside down. As it collapsed in upon itself it opened up first one chasm, and then another. The day's mirror cracked, slowly at first and then at a terrifying speed. All the bright world exploded and behind it was nothing but vertigo, coming at me like the wind in the desert.

When I was twelve my godmother told me: 'Nobody can explain it, child. All you can say is that it's there.'

She was rubbing her small hand across her stomach. Her round head with the short hair would not stop nodding. She lifted her chin and swallowed down the glass of white wine she had just poured.

When she got up from the armchair into which she had sunk, her whole body was trembling, she was upright but shaking all over. She went to the fridge where she had found the bottle. She took out the cork and reached for the glass and filled it to the brim.

'No,' I said, following her every movement. 'No. No.'

She didn't answer. She drank it down very fast. She smiled as if relieved. She came back and sat in the armchair.

'It's as if some animal got in there one day and won't go away. When it moves, it hurts. It's hard to stop it moving.'

I imagined a seahorse, pink and snake-like. At the bottom of her arm you could see the swollen scar where the veins had been cut. To rehabilitate the hand and wrist they advise you to play with a little rubber ball.

'Don't cry,' said my godmother. She put out her hand and stroked my hair with the palm of her hand. 'You're not to blame. It's not your fault.'

'I was supposed to keep an eye on you,' I murmured. 'Mum and Dad asked me to. When they went for their run, they hid the pills. They forgot about the wine.'

My godmother smiled.

'Just as well you can't think of everything. But I shouldn't have woken up. It doesn't matter, I'm going to go to sleep again. You don't need to tell them I got up.'

She leaned on the armrests to raise herself from the armchair. In her crumpled pyjamas she looked very skinny and shrunken. She went back to her room where the shutters were down and fell on to the bed without closing the door. Alone in the empty living-room, I wept. It was summer and ten o'clock in the morning.

Suddenly the streets emptied. As I turned the pages of the newspaper unread I tried to focus my mind. The seahorse was uncurling itself in my belly. It swelled. It took my breath away. I wanted to be sick.

The photos in the newspaper scrambled together. A black mash stuck to my fingers. I closed the pages slowly, carefully. And began to cry. My tears flooded out much too fast, splashing down on to my hands.

I couldn't stop. I buried my head in my bag and pulled out my address book. I squeezed it between my fingers.

'Where shall I go?'

My body had become too big for me, a heavy painful lump that my spirit had no strength to move. In a measured fashion I pushed the table away from me. The *patronne* was looking my way furiously. The phone was at the back on the left.

'Where to go, where to go, where to go.'

I did the easiest thing. I called my cousin.

On the glass door at the back of the café, the letters *Toilettes-Téléphone* showed through in gold. On the right a half-closed door gave on to a black recess. There was a strong smell of disinfectant.

I leaned against the tiled wall, next to the telephone, searching in my pocket for the coins. I looked at my shoes, my laces were all undone. From the inside pocket of my jacket I took out my dark glasses. I dialled the number from memory.

'Hullo, it's me.'

'Are you okay?'

I answered with a little hiccup.

'Hey, how are you?'

'Not very well,' I whispered.

'So I see.'

'What shall I do?'

'Where are you?'

'At Répu.'

'Come straight away. I'm here.'

'But how can I? I can't stop crying.'

'Take a taxi.'

'I can't.'

'The metro then.'

'I really can't.'

'Then use your legs and walk, silly.'

I blew my nose on a scrap of paper. I put the phone down and an avalanche of small coins fell out. Oh good, three euros. I picked up the money and went back into the café. I went out leaving the three euros and my newspaper on the table and the *patronne* scooped them up with an air of indifference.

I took the Rue du Faubourg-du-Temple, then the Boulevard de Belleville. I walked slowly so as not to disturb the seahorse which had curled up and was slumbering, as big as my fist, on the level of my solar plexus. Crowds clogged the pavements. Thousands of heads floated by like little blind corks. I tried to make my way through them, tried not to see them as I moved forward, letting my blank gaze trail in the air.

Grey skin is like a veil, violet flesh is streaked with white veins, bones are made of ivory and pink hearts have the texture of sponge. It is extremely unpleasant seeing through the appearance of things and under someone's skin.

Crowds have one expression, cruel and fixed. You let yourself be trapped by a look. You let yourself be carried off and shut away in a place of silence. There your eyes may be ripped out, your tongue cut off, and your fingers hammered until the little bones splinter. The walls are splashed with thick clots of blood. Words are the worst kind of dog, they drag us along despite ourselves to somewhere we didn't want to go, they obsess us, they don't let us have a moment's rest, a moment's rest.

But before that? Before that is another place altogether. Memory blanks things out methodically. It has several floors, sealed off from one another and there is no passage joining them. One of them is hell. When you fall in, at the very instant you lose your footing, you forget everything, even what light is like. But once you are back in the world you retain only a faint memory of being shut up. It resonates like the dull echo of pain.

I was counting my footsteps, from one to twenty. When I got to twenty I began again. The music of the numbers rocked the seahorse to sleep. I hummed them to keep him from moving in the front of my stomach. I took great care not to stop singing. Along the Rue du

Faubourg, as I went by, the shops were opening up like flowers. The city enfolded me in its calyx.

As I walked, a name came and lodged itself in my mind. Behind the name was a bed in a hotel bedroom, and, lying on that bed I was watching a boy take his clothes off. He was half-undressed, I watched him, leaning back on the pillows.

It occurred to me that I'd like to return to that hotel, for the few hours which were ahead of me. But the moment had gone and the boy had left. There is no point hoping to repeat moments that have vanished, any more than there is any point regretting them. No use being sad about it, nor especially happy either, come to that. Love is a deserted place, an abandoned room, nothing gained, nothing lost. I tried to remember what he looked like, but only words came to me. His name came back along with a sadness that wouldn't go away, but affected me like nausea.

On the Boulevard de Belleville the market had put up its noisy stands. You edged your way through a narrow opening between the stalls. Behind the stall-holders shouting their wares, bruised fruit, rotting vegetables were crushed in the gutters, waiting to be picked up by the poor and the down-and-outs. Tears poured down my cheeks. A warm flood, it escaped from the fountain of my being.

'Mustn't cry so much, my girl,' said a big woman in an apron from her place behind the boxes of vegetables.

Farther off, two men in blue stood back to let me through, both looking at me pityingly as I walked past.

I got to the end of the boulevard, finally I arrived. I pushed open the huge wooden door. Under the archway the paving-stones soaked up the damp shade. A large enamel sign advertised a firm: *La Belle Vie*, which had set up inside the courtyard. A staircase went up from inside the archway on the right. Light-brown steps curved up, polished by the feet of the tenants.

I knocked several times with my fist before he came and opened the door, hairy, familiar, just woken up, enveloped in his ragged dressing-gown.

'Come in,' he said, his hand on my shoulder.

He made me sit on the bed. My legs were closed, my knees straight, my back hunched, and my hands joined together in front of my nose. I sniffed, I was wearing my black jacket, and my bag was next to me. A sorry figure abandoned at a bus stop.

'Okay, you can stop crying now, you've got here.'

'Nowhere,' I groaned, 'I haven't got anywhere.' I put my head down.

'It'll get better... No good shaking your head, it'll get better, I tell you.'

But it was clear to him that nothing was getting better, and he added:

'Come on then, what's the matter?'

'I wish I knew. It comes on me all at once. Usually I can cope, but this morning I can't, I'm tired.'

'All the same something must have happened, even something not important...'

'No, nothing's changed. Nothing new. Except that I'm tired.'

He lowered his head. He looked at his shoes.

'Don't make excuses. You're no heavier than anyone else.'

'Do you think so?'

'Lightweight people', he observed, lighting a cigarette, 'are a thousand times worse than heavyweights. Because lightweights are a pain in the backside. Remember that, my dear. And weigh it up.'

'I'm going to make a hot coffee. In the meantime, take this.'

He rummaged in his pocket. He took out a packet of pale blue tablets.

'And this.'

He took a book from his desk and held it out.

'It's a story about a depressive who decides to go on his travels. In short, he goes off. All too soon he realizes he's made a mistake, that his life is even more of a struggle when he is a long way from home. He is so unhappy that finally he has a heart attack. In his hotel room, all by himself. It's good, it's funny, you'll see.'

Mechanically, I took the tablets and the book from him.

'Are you sure I'm not a nuisance?'

He shrugged his shoulders and went out of the room.

I stretched out meekly and pulled up over me the duvet that lay in a heap over my toes. I brought my knees up to my chest and listened. The sound of trays clattering, bowls being moved around, the breathing of the fridge opening and closing, spoons dropping on the tiled floor. The thousand small kitchen noises mingled with Frank's soliloquies.

The noise lay over my stomach like a compress. The sun came through the shutters in cut slices of light and fell on the cluttered desk. Three packets of Winston without filters, a small notebook, a quill pen, biros, wooden pencils that needed sharpening but no pencil-sharpener, a wallet, a credit card, cotton trousers rolled up in a ball with a polo sweater, a dried-out and chewed toothbrush, photos, a pile of books, a box of

Doliprane, a box of Lysanxia, a box of Spasfon. Bandages. Just in case. Music cassettes. A sock.

All the small muscles in my body relaxed, like so many sleeping canals. I fell asleep. When Frank came back, with a bowl in his hand, I was fast asleep with my jacket on, my arms by my side, my nose in the pillow. He put the bowl at the foot of the bed.

When I opened my eyes again, the stallholders were taking down their stands, in a sea of lettuce stumps and rotten fruit.

I sat up, pulling my jacket around me. I saw the bowl of coffee at the end of the bed and got up. I glanced through the half-open door. He was sitting at the table in his dressing-gown. Pencil in hand, he was reading a book and making notes while a cigarette burned in the ash-tray.

I was at peace, contemplating him in the midday sunshine, when the ringing of the telephone shattered the silence. Frank bounded towards the phone and saw me, standing framed in the doorway.

'Don't answer it!'

The phone went on ringing for some time in the little room. When the answer-phone kicked in, Frank leaned over the speaker. Nothing. Beep. No message.

'There, you see,' he said triumphantly.

'What do I see?'

'If it was to tell me something they would have left a message.'

'So?'

'So, they just wanted to know if I was there, or annoy me incidentally if I answered. But I didn't answer it. I'm not such a fool.'

The telephone understood. Silent, like a beaten animal, full of mute reproach and hypocritical threats, it remained immobile.

'I'm off to get dressed,' said Frank, going into his bedroom. 'Take a bowl from the table. The coffee's hot. I've just made some more.'

I helped myself. I stared hard at the coffee, right to the bottom of my bowl. I saw the sugar implode in the hot liquid, curl and break into little pieces. I thought of disappearing, of being removed, of exile. I wanted to die. I placed my hand on my stomach and started to weep again, huge tears, like rain in a Flanders summer. Great waves splashing down slowly into the damp.

'Aaaah!' Frank breathed, coming out of his room, half bent over. He had put on some greyish beige trousers and was finishing buttoning them up. 'Aaaah, my belly's killing me.'

He lifted his eyes from his belt and gave me a look of disgust.

'Again? You still crying? Are you kidding?'

He rubbed the palm of his hand against his brow in a weary sort of way.

'Do you want me to go?'

I opened my eyes wide, chin raised, looking at the ceiling, unshed tears in my eyes, a real salty lake.

'Stay here, you little fool, stay here. But make something to eat instead of moaning. You'll find some stuff in the fridge. I'm going to buy the paper and some fags.'

As an accompaniment to the pasta I boiled some tomatoes. Their skin suddenly burst and they rose, like balloons, to the simmering surface of the water. I took the saucepan off the stove and tipped the hot water down the sink. I edged the tomatoes gently on to a plate. As they got cold the skin would get too tight and would retract on the pulp. All I had to do was take the fruit between my thumb and forefinger and pull a little bit to get completely bare tomatoes that I would cut into crescent shapes. In the bottom of the pan I placed two spoonfuls of butter which I allowed to melt. When the butter began to hiss, I threw in some basil. I watched the thick leaves melt in the yellowy juices and become absorbed, without losing their dense green colour.

The kitchen was so small that if you turned round you could lay the table, keep an eye on the cooking, and wash the dishes all at the same time. To reach the dish-mop or the spices you had to raise your arm. If you got on your knees you could clean the fridge. Adjust the seasoning, add salt or pepper. The kitchen is a happy little world unto itself.

'Want some more pasta?' I enquired.

He pushed back his plate and looked at me quizzically. My face was smooth and serene, as when you emerge after a peaceful night. All you could see of the morning's tears was one slightly swollen eyelid. What a waste of time. He got up from the table.

'I'll make some coffee.'

From the other side of the wall I could hear him moving around in the cubby-hole. I crossed my legs and lit a cigarette.

When he came back to sit opposite me, he caught hold of my hand and pinched the ends of my fingers.

'You've started biting your nails?'

'Now and again. When I'm unhappy.'

Frank let go my hand and sighed.

'Do you think we are more unhappy than other people?'

'Who do you mean by us?'

'You, me, for instance.'

I laughed.

'No, not more unhappy. But we think we are going to be. We shout louder and sooner. We bawl like polecats before we are even hurt. It doesn't stop the blows. It gives them a certain rhythm.'

'What are you doing this evening?' enquired Frank.

'Nothing.'

Though I had stopped crying I still wasn't feeling very good about myself. I felt about as strong as a cut-out paper doll that you keep upright by standing it against a matchstick.

'I don't know how I'm going to get home,' I added, thinking aloud; it boded ill for me returning to my messy apartment. 'I don't know if I'll have the strength to last a night all on my own.'

'Stay here, you can sleep on the couch. I'm going out tonight, you can watch television while you're waiting. I shouldn't be back late. And I'll leave you my number. Don't you need to go home and get your things?'

'What things? I've got everything I need in my bag, my address book, my credit card. You can lend me a toothbrush. If I need anything else I can always buy some socks at Monoprix.'

Frank raised his eyes to heaven.

'At Monoprix. The life you lead. And afterwards she'll tell me she's tired. The day you find a way of filling your apartment with something you need—some bloke, a book, a stamp collection—that day I swear you won't be so tired.'

'I'm scared,' said my godmother, 'I'm scared.'

Yet she had a husband, children, an apartment, possessions. In her flat all the shutters were down, the curtains drawn.

'I'm scared,' was all she said whenever I met her in the dark passageway and caught hold her hand.

She would pull her hand away and go back to her room. It was very mysterious, that dark apartment and that bedroom where she did nothing but sleep.

It was certain she hadn't found anyone who would prevent her going back to her apartment. And on her own she hadn't had the strength to escape. So she had been caught like a rat in a trap, incapable of lifting the door of her cage.

'Okay, I agree then. Are you sure it's not a problem for you?'

'No problem at all. In any case no one comes here any more. I am such a gloomy sod in the end I put everyone's back up.'

'No girlfriend?'

'Never again.'

'Don't say that, it's silly.'

'No, it's the truth. I've wasted enough time and energy and I know what I'm talking about. Frankly, I prefer to be on my own. Then everyone's better off.'

'I am, perhaps,' I concluded. 'I don't know about you. What can I do between now and this evening?'

'I can safely predict snoozing, reading, perhaps a bit of television...'

'Good,' I said, 'Thank you.'

'You're welcome.'

'All the same, you are a bit of a life-saver.'

'That's right. Put it in the Plus column.'

Outside the afternoon was triumphant. The sun was playing its trumpet. We two were sitting with our cold coffees in front of us, leafing through the shared newpaper. The summer poured sweet warmth upon us. I took a deep breath. The seahorse shrivelled up and was crushed, stifled by the sheer force of my diaphragm. It tied itself in knots, somewhere in my stomach. It disappeared into the turmoil of cells in my body.

'Are you feeling better?' asked Frank, raising his eyes.

'Yes, I think it's gone.'

He put his hand on my shoulder.

'You see, you mustn't let it get to you. It's like stomach-ache, it always passes off in the end.'

I thought: 'Almost always.'

But I said nothing. I was calm. I didn't particularly want to talk any more.

Refined

Daniel Boulanger

'Come in!'

'Monsieur Caval? Telegram.'

Caval put down his cigar and read: 'Aunt Suzy passed away Geneva wishes you attend cremation Paris. Family mourning loss. Love.'

Caval immediately got on the phone to Geneva. 'I accept on one condition: that I don't go to the columbarium in the hearse.' Aunt Suzy had left enough money to do things properly. Caval followed the deceased in a Cadillac belonging to the funeral directors. The first thing he did was light a cigar. The delightful ride, sun high in the sky, the scented havana, a heavenly blue Paris, Caval was happy with life.

'This way!'

He jumped.

'We've arrived.'

He had forgotten Tante Suzy, the crematorium, Père-Lachaise, and the expression he ought to assume.

He threw away the rest of his cigar and addressed the person who was speaking to him: 'Oh God!'

'I understand,' said the man in black. 'Do you wish to see her cremated?'

'No thanks.'

'Do you wish to wait in the funeral parlour, and we will play you some sacred music?'

'Thank you. I do not.'

'I understand. May I make a suggestion? The ceremony lasts as long as it takes to eat a meal. It is nearly twelve. As you go out, you have on the left-hand side, the *Petit Lachaise*, very well-managed, clean, quality food. Come back in an hour and a half.'

Caval looked at the man in black with the mournful expression, his eyes and shoulders, and something else which he could not quite fathom hidden deep in his nature.

'Thanks,' said Caval, moving off like an automaton down the path the man had indicated.

At the *Petit Lachaise* Caval chose grilled sausage to start.

'Well-grilled?'

'Yes,' he said, and suddenly Aunt Suzy came to mind.

He was still thinking about her when the man in black came into the restaurant.

'If you don't mind, I'll share your table. I've set everything in train. We have plenty of time. Is that nice?'

He pointed to the sausage.

'Very.'

'They've let it burn a bit,' the man in black went on. 'One should come a bit later, towards two o'clock, after the flames have died down, but we don't have much choice.'

Tante Suzy came and went in between the courses. Caval felt good anyway and the man in black was drinking steadily.

'Didn't I tell you? It's a nice little place.'

'I shall come again,' Caval assured him, not thinking about anything beyond that.

They went on to seasonal fruits, coffee, and spirits.

'Oh I couldn't...' said the man in black.

'I should be offended,' Caval insisted, paying the bill.

As he went out, the man in black looked at the sky. Caval did too.

'Getting cloudy.'

'Looks like rain.'

Then they discussed politics a little as they went back up the cemetery path.

'Here we are,' said the man in black finally. His expression had not changed for one moment. 'Let's go in.'

Caval followed him to the asbestos table that had been taken out of the gaping oven. Two assistants were finishing raking up the still-smoking remains and putting them into a little box placed on an iron chair. Caval's gaze was fixed on some bits of bone which looked like pumice-stone, little pebbles with holes in, ochre, white, and yellow. They would have to cool completely before going up to the marble library where the books are little urns of ashes. The man in black hurried things along, to make it easier. Caval scarcely heard him as with some emotion, his hat in his hand, he said to his assistants in a grave voice:

'Cool Madame off in the garden. Monsieur is a friend.'

A Little Accident

Colette

Saturday afternoon, a motorcar and a horse and trap were drawn up on opposite sides of the road in the Rue Daunou, against the pavement. A long automobile with an open top, steered by its owner from the boulevard, drove at speed in between the two vehicles. There was a small strip of road left, wide enough for a wheelbarrow, too narrow for a donkey-cart: the cab taking me from the Rue de la Paix to the boulevards pitched in, with the kind of blind wilfulness and impulsive disregard for danger and the laws of physics we find so marvellous in the cinema—where the enchanted taxi swims through floods, plunges straight into a chalet in Normandy, and comes out of a skylight in the attic.

The two side impacts on the cab were hefty, and although I was the very model of reserve, bleeding modestly from forehead and nose into my handkerchief, fifty onlookers, ten vehicles, and three policemen stopped in an instant.

The variety of their sounds all combined would have greatly intrigued a person much more badly injured than I was. As I mingled with the curious, I gathered that the owner of the car, a foreigner, somewhat slow of speech, was being generally blamed, thanks to the cab-driver who, fiery, quick-tempered, and able to talk the hind leg off a donkey, had already entered the fray, calling him a clumsy fool, a liar, and a spy. When they heard the word 'spy' three elegant ladies exploded. One poked her parasol as if it were a goad at the foreigner and fumed:

'Why do they come over here, instead of staying in their own country!'

Voices in the crowd, swelled and echoed:

'—come over here . . . stay in their own country!'

Thus encouraged, the lady began the familiar series of daunting and irrefutable truths:

'In the first place, if there weren't so many foreigners in Paris there wouldn't be so many cars in the streets!'

And random voices from the crowd took up the cry:

'—not so many foreigners in the streets...not so many cars in Paris!'

Then the three women chorused:

'Send him to the Front! What's a big strong man like that doing sitting there in his car stopping everyone getting past? To the Front with him! He can explain himself later.'

A fine-looking chorus-leader, ruddy-cheeked, broad-shouldered, in civilian clothes, pushed his way through to the driver of the car and harangued him as though he were on stage:

'Indeed, Monsieur, we are surprised to find you here, in your waistcoat and trilby! If you belong to a friendly nation, an ally, as, so it seemed to me, you claimed just now, should you not be inside its frontiers, armed and ready for battle?'

The car-driver finally managed to splutter:

'I am not claiming anything, Monsieur! I am Italian, that's all. And I am forty-eight years old! And as for you there in your morning coat, you who...you...'

That was exactly what our man was waiting for! He smiled his perfect smile, with one look rallying the attention of the ladies present, and said:

'I'm fifty-one years old, Monsieur! What do you say to that?'

Having waited a moment, no doubt to be asked for his beauty tips, he went off in search of another traffic accident which would give him the opportunity to reassert, not only his patriotic sentiments, but his triumphantly youthful appearance.

Meanwhile the driver of the damaged trap was handing over to one of the three policemen personal documents with photos to back them up, evidence of his unassailable past history. The second policeman, suspicious and distracted, was listening to the protests of the foreign motorist, whose wing had been wrecked, and the highly-coloured language, rich in epithets, of the brilliant jouster to whom I had entrusted my fate half an hour earlier. The third policeman had already covered, in a pleasant, curling hand, two long pages from a notebook. He wrote and wrote, inspired, withdrawn from the world. It was to him that I addressed myself:

'May I go now, Monsieur l'agent?'

He did not raise his studious brow:

'Yes, Madame, you carry on: there are too many people here already... You have no evidence to give about the accident? No one has asked you any questions?'

'Oh no, Monsieur l'agent, I was on the receiving end.'

'You were a victim? . . .'

He lifted his eyes from the notebook and considered the bruise on my nose and the cut on my forehead:

'Ah yes,' he muttered abstractedly. 'A classic motor accident. The least little bump and people think that everyone is dead, but in the end, as you can see yourself: it's less than nothing, less than nothing . . .'

If it were Sunday

Annie Saumont

My hand slides down the rail. That man is looking at me. I turn to you and say really Ada you look a fright with your hair like that this morning. You toss your short plaits, tied with bands. You smile and say you'll do your hair better on your wedding day, on Saint Whoever's day, you suppress a giggle, you claim you haven't even got a boyfriend. And what about the son of the woman in the bakery who gives you an apple tart when his mother's back is turned? And what about Gérard? You protest. Gérard is more like an older brother, when he kisses you, you don't like it very much, his beard tickles.

Again you giggle. You say how hot it is, you say you can't breathe my back is damp my dress is all crumpled. And you whisper to me that the people sitting in the carriage or standing up in silence look like zombies. Even more *sotto voce* you say, except the one by the door, Thérèse, that super-cool guy who can't stop staring at you. Outside, the wall flashes past, purple shadows in the gaps where the plaster is blistering, signs, white circles triangles arrows the sudden dazzle of naked bulbs, a flashing light, he thinks you are sexy you tell me.

The wall, abruptly cut off, the poster, a sunny beach with *Fang Citron* in a frosted glass brandished by a handsome young man. On the platform people are jostling one another, boarding the train, crushing our toes. If it were Sunday morning we should be going for a walk in the woods. Our arms would be round each other's waists. We should be smiling, fresh, relaxed. This evening my legs are tired, we've walked miles, not through woods but from one counter to the next in the department stores going from one floor to another examining all the displays then out in the street running for the metro, me pulling you along, come on, quick, quick. You collapsed on a seat on the platform, moaning what's the matter, Thérése, don't be so daft, there was no need to rush.

We two so close to each other holding tight to the hand-rail, a jolt and you are thrown against me your hair across my cheek, your laughter on my neck. You tell me it's not good for us to spend too long looking at things we covet in shops you dream of being able to point to something and say that and that and that as well, send it all to this address. Usually on Saturdays you choose a visit to the Planetarium as your special treat. You can't possibly want to own a nebula, you've copied down names of stars in your notebook, you'd like to be called Vega or Orionis. You say you are sure you saw that man this afternoon in the jewellery department in front of the satin-lined showcase you say I brushed against him, he smiled, perhaps he has a present for me in his pocket.

I pull a face, Ada you're crazy, that man's going home, he lives in Rue de Tolbiac or on Boulevard Masséna, that's why he's on the same metro as us, will you never stop making up stories. A small house in the suburbs a patch of grass in front of the steps, when we lay in the plantain you pretended to be sleeping in the middle of fields that stretched from the other side of the dunes to the sandy shore. In the end Gérard and I believed you, breathing more easily, listening to the sea, forgetting the building with the flaking stone, the rusty railings with the For Sale sign on. A spindle hedge, the tree dead, a clothes-line tied to its last branch cutting off the corner of the yard near the sharp-scented black-currants, the twisted elder, its roots lifting the slabs of the steps. All of us pretended to be quite at home, relaxed, a neighbour might have leaned over the hedge. One by one Gérard extracted the bits of grass caught in his beard and his hair so long it reached his shoulders. All that hair disgusts me, I am glad you dislike Gérard's caresses. Gérard makes you a necklace out of rose-hips, suggests some star names for you, Schedir Rigel Aldebaran. At nights I am afraid Gérard will touch you while you are asleep, I stretch out be-tween you on the wretched mattress that's been left in the bedroom, we haven't done any damage. Gérard is good at forcing locks.

The man has taken a step closer, the metro creaks, I take a step back hanging on to your wrist I am squashing you against the elderly lady whose chin has disappeared into her shabby velvet coat, the man leans against the window, his suit is immaculate, he is wear-ing a wedding ring, shiny boots, a Chanel tie, you mutter, that man's so loaded he doesn't know what to do with it. You and me, by selling our needles on the market we earn twenty centimes on each packet laid out in the tray that bruises our breasts. The strap has left a mark on the back of your neck.

Walking along by the houses in the district where your parents lived you weren't saying very much, I followed you into the thickly carpeted hall, you told me to wait there a moment. I could hear you through the wall, Mum it's my friend Thérèse, she works, she runs a business she's asked me to help her, haberdashery knitting wools, don't worry Mum we'll share her place, my tiny attic room on the top-floor is metamorphosed into an airy, comfortable studio flat, in your dreams Ada, the little house is a castle, the miserable elder blooms on the edge of a park, a puddle becomes a lake in which the sky floats and drifts. That day we were alone in the rotunda of the Planetarium, they projected the galaxy on to the great dome just for us. Our faces gazing up, me turning my head and seeing the vein in your neck pulsating so close to me. The universe already five billion years old, the life in us, its eternal tumult, suddenly in me a great tug of anguish, of longing so intense I nearly cry out. Then I grew resentful and impatient behind the living-room door, you went on, Mum, how can you judge without knowing anything about her, she's my friend, I tell you, her dad's a (teacher? doctor? lawyer?), your voice was shaking, listen Mum, her mother's dead.

There am I in the corridor, sweating, waiting for the hmm, well, all right. Later I persuaded you it didn't matter about her approval, we lived together we sold skeins of wool, reels of thread, elasticated, gros-grain. We said, come and buy ladies and gentlemen it's in aid of the blind. Some people make their fortune as if it were nothing, no trouble at all, gambling or in business, imagine, if it were a Sunday we'd go to the races we'd have read *Paris-Turf,* we'd find a wad of notes pinned together in the grass in the paddock, we'd lay a bet on Éclair Blanc and there he is the winner, galloping across the finishing-line.

We studied the ads in the paper, we have to work, make up your mind. Gérard used to say, you can always get by, and you folding down the pages, usherette shelf-stacker telephonist post-office worker, if it were a Sunday and not raining we'd go into the country and eat our sandwiches. You'd be called Altaïr or Deneb. Gérard says work's a kind of slavery, he says it's a curse, Gérard refuses. Gérard manages, don't ask me how, you believe him when he tells you he's come into some money, from his grandfather who died of cancer, that's why he can afford meals of seaweed and soya for himself and for us and buys himself flashy kaftans your mum wouldn't like them. I held my breath. A silence. She said, you certainly choose your friends, don't you. My arm tensed. Knocked against the ashtray.

We've passed Pont-Neuf. You poke me with your elbow. There's the man looking at me. I brush your cheek. He's come closer, his hand shifts down the rail. I remove mine. At your parents' house I kept aloof, trying to follow your explanations, already exasperated. Then—it was last year—a suburban street the privet hedge high railings, the house, I screamed, Gérard get lost, Gérard wanted to make love to you, I'll tell your parents, Ada, don't go supposing they would like him. You shrug, it's because of your parents that you asked who my father was and where he lived, Gérard was sprawling over the dry lawn saying, Ada I'll teach you the meaning of joy. Lying against me with your face on my arm you were asking me about my father, your mother's dead but your father—I could have said that he was dead too, I didn't want to tell you anything, when I saw him after such a long time first I couldn't believe it, Mum, it can't be true it can't be, you must be joking, and she, he used to be a lot better-looking. Mum with fine features and quite pretty, he heavy with flab, his blood thick, Ada, that's what men get like, your Gérard will have a pot-belly, folds under his chin, cheeks criss-crossed with little veins, like my dad, and mum in a daydream, he was handsome wide-shouldered narrow hips, he loved dancing, at that time dances always ended with a competition, the spectators chose their favourite couple from amongst the candidates. Mum also said, he and I went in for the competition, once we won first prize, I've even got a piece of paper a certificate, they asked us to waltz on our own on the dance-floor, your father could go on for ever.

My dad sat at the table, groaning, opening the newspaper reading out the items about armed robberies rapes, and me staring at the wall trying to be somewhere else to calm down, he'll go in ten minutes. You ask me what I'm thinking about, Ada. I say nothing. I shan't tell you that one day, I was seven, I stole a bag of chocolates from the display and the woman in the grocery, dirty little girl, damned thief, grabbing my arm and shaking me, it's in her blood. You in the sitting-room, it's my friend Thérèse. Me behind the wall noticing a tiny black spot in the corner, a spider killed by the swipe of a duster. Yes her mother's dead, her father, oh I don't know, he went off. You added, to America. And you continued, I think he's the director of a bank or a factory over there. Me behind the door, stiff and tense, you insisting, her mum's dead. I was touching the ashtray on the little table. I hoped your mum was going to say, dinner's ready, let her stay.

I was sitting with my back to the sink in the kitchen in our house. Dad had brought two bags of chips and sausages in greaseproof paper. He said don't we make a nice picture, two old friends sharing a meal. Then all that was left on the table was the greasy wrappers and the mustard pot. I didn't move. The almost imperceptible ticking of the clock. He'd got permission to see me every Sunday he yawned uncovering his yellow teeth the decay of the molars the inside of his mouth a purplish pink like the flesh of fat figs opened up by the rain. Raising his eyes he registered surprise, didn't I have anything to tell him, haha, no boyfriends yet? At your age you don't tell your secrets, a click of the tongue, you're a fine girl now, come over here, don't be silly, he assured me I used to climb on to his knee come here what a stupid idea to put trousers on you, he said I would have looked better in a short skirt it's your mother isn't it dresses you up like that, pulling me towards him his finger through my belt, well, shout as much as you like, your mother is scared of me she won't come down.

Men. That's what they're like. Gérard. The baker's son. My dad. His eager fingers fumbling with the ring on the zip. Mum was leaning over the banisters saying it's time, he let me go reluctantly and said, sniggering, see you Sunday. He goes out into the street. Men in the street. Men in the metro. That one looking at us. You rummage in your coat pocket you take out a crumpled ticket you remind me you have to get out at Porte d'Italie to go and say hi to your cousin Alberte who gives you money when you go and see her. You add in an undertone, that man is waiting for me to leave you before he invites you to a restaurant, you pretend he's going to ask me to come on holiday with him, a cruise, take me too, you murmur. We'd be on a huge ship, the orchestra would be playing jazz we'd eat all we want, the other passengers would be seasick.

Us two sunning ourselves, salt on our lips, eyelids fluttering, your body on mine, not speaking. One day when I'm rich we'll go away we shan't need Cousin Alberte any more. You lean over, see you this evening Thérèse, and I whisper, come back quickly. I'll be outside the home under the archway near the bench for the old people in the hospice. Suddenly I'll hear your footsteps hurrying. We used to go walking late into the night talking about how beautiful the world was. Gérard says the whole earth could be a garden of love we'd walk wherever we wanted and never tire of admiring it.

In the Home the Sisters of La Pitié are afraid of the dark, afraid on our behalf, they say, after dusk bad desires awaken evil creeps up to the threshold, that's why they have in their hands keys and chains to lock us in as soon as twilight comes. When we lived in my attic room we never worried about the time. But we had no

more money for rent and often nothing to eat. Sometimes you have crazy plans, you'll go travelling. With
Gérard. For a whole evening you discuss it. You'd get
sore feet Ada you mustn't go. You are fine with me
I look after you I let you dream of everything they told
you about when you were little, happiness is quite
simple, in a loving family, mother gets the meal
ready, father about to come home, tired, smiling already. On Sundays he reads his newspaper, does a few
jobs in the garden, snoozes in front of the television.
Rest, rites. Obeying the rules. I took the ashtray, your
mum was about to say invite her to dinner then, she
talked, she was asking can you tell me where she comes
from ? From beyond the pale. From some scabby street
where the gutters overflow.

They were on the pavement. He had his back to the
wall. Mum just above the gutter. She usually took
refuge upstairs while the visit lasted. But I had yelled
out I called her, when she got downstairs, still stuck on
his chair, he was holding me between his legs squeezing
my backside he had pulled my trousers down, you're a
fine girl. Mum told me to go up to her room he let me
go. He went out she followed him, their voices raised,
violent, what a fuss about nothing a father is allowed to
have a look at his own daughter. That's when the van
mounted the pavement. I listened to the cries then the

howling of the sirens. I kept telling myself it's him, it's him they're taking off, dead, run over, I was lying on my bed my face in the pillow, the back of my neck stiff with cramp, the damp cloth against my cheek, at the very worst they are both dead, I didn't move, I felt better. Someone came, handed me my coat I found myself in the street. It was the evening I looked up so as not to miss any of the wonderful sky. Never before had I seen it so brilliant so calm. Someone pushed me into a car they took me to hospital.

Years later, the rules of the home forbade any hanging around outside at night, you and I decided to go and stargaze in the Planetarium. A solemn voice talked to us solemnly about novae, cephaids. I saw your rapt face in the half light. Don't dawdle on the way back Ada, the nuns'll make a real fuss. Be in time for Prayers. You smile at me. The man in the metro is gazing at me. They will say Lord in your great mercy holy protection your children assembled your grace tomorrow once more. I shall be on my knees next to you and you'll be waving your ten franc note around, alms from your cousin Alberte. One more time I shall say forgive us our sins as we forgive—

One day he reappeared, he asked me for some cash, I was coming back from the cemetery I said he could starve to death in front of me, that even then—He said

I'm your father don't forget. I shouted, you've just left prison. If these women expel us from the Home, these bloody women, where shall we sleep, Ada. Once again we shall be looking for empty houses, in the suburbs, often to get in we break a pane of glass you know that costs a lot if you're caught. My dad sighed well yes, I stole. Your mother there dead and mutilated on the pavement in front of me, that made me go off the rails. I said lowering my voice it wasn't the first time, in our area people know about it, he sniggered, Thérèse show me your hands they look like mine your thumb wide and separated from the other fingers, hands cut out for nicking things, you can tell straight away, tell me, surely you have once or twice—The sweets. The ashtray. First I took it from the side table and then put it back. Your mother said, we want to protect you, Ada. And over there in the Home it's for your own good.

Now my father's laugh. It means that one day I too—that's how it is in our family, from father to son or father to daughter. Ada stay with me, you argue that you are right to be nice to your cousin. But please don't stay too late, we'll go and have a mint Vittel before it's time for supper. The surveillante on duty will point out that those two always together we should—The train stops I say very quickly that if I'm not standing by the railings tonight near the split tree—but you are gone, the doors close, only another three stations till the terminus. The man near the window has shifted his position slightly, I see him in profile, he seems to have forgotten me. I wish the metro would carry on for a long time, for ever, I won't move, scarcely breathing, I'll remember those moments of hope, Mum it's my friend Thérèse, yes, she's here and if you wanted to—There would still be time enough for a gentle voice to answer what a good idea, let's keep her. I smile, the lights on the platform dazzle me and hurt me as I leap towards the door.

The man gets out just after me. He puts his hand on my shoulder. I don't resist. He guides me to the stairs the exit the street. People walking on the pavement look as though they are occupied by gloomy thoughts. Look it's raining. Let's forget about our cruise, Ada. You don't feel comfortable on ships, you can't escape. The sky in a great hemisphere we'll go and see it in the Planetarium. We'll go back there Ada. Don't follow Gérard if he wants you to come travelling with him, if he talks about a propitious conjunction of the planets, about fields carpeted with soft grass on summer nights full of stars, he makes it up, he talks rubbish, be wary of men Ada. This one is pointing to a door, over there, open wide with a rather grubby flag on top. He is stopping where the street and the boulevard intersect. We might have been hairdressers, secretaries, punch-card operators, it's Thérèse, my friend Thérèse, we are going to be working together she's good at all sorts of things, she's serious, her mother's dead. Ada listen, we'll manage, I promise we'll find something. An abandoned house and further off the leafy trees, the sky between the branches, a good squat, freedom tenderness. Happiness, Ada. The man is squeezing my right arm above the elbow where the skin is tender. I shove my left hand into my pocket. He and I are stuck at the crossing. While he is looking at the traffic lights all I have to do is lean slightly towards the open grid and with swift, skilful fingers, throw his wallet in.

Facino Cane

Honoré de Balzac

At that time I was living in a little street you have probably never heard of, the Rue de Lesdiguières. It starts in the Rue Saint-Antoine, opposite a fountain near Place de la Bastille, and comes out in the Rue de la Cerisaie. My desire for learning had driven me to a garret where I worked at night, spending my days in a nearby library, the one that used to belong to Monsieur. I lived frugally, embracing all the conditions of a monastic life, so necessary when one is working. On fine days I would, at most, go for a walk along the Boulevard Bourdon. One sole passion, and one only, made me forsake my studious habits; but might you not still call it 'study'? I went to observe the local customs, the people and their characters. No better turned-out than the working men and indifferent to all decorum, I did not put them on their guard towards me; I was able to mingle with them freely, watch them clinching deals or arguing as they left work. This faculty of observation had already become second nature, I delved deep into the inner man without ignoring the outer; or, should I say, I grasped the external details so well that I was immediately able to go beyond them. It gave me the capacity to live the life of the person whom I was observing, allowing me to take his place, just as the dervish in the *Thousand and One Nights* took on the body and soul of those people over whom he uttered certain words.

When, between eleven o'clock and midnight, I met a working man and his wife coming back together from the Ambigu-Comique, I would amuse myself by following them from the Boulevard of the Pont-aux-Choux to the Boulevard Beaumarchais. These good people would at first discuss the show they had just seen. Little by little they would get round to talking about their finances. The mother would drag her child along, ignoring his complaints and questions. The man and his wife would be working out what they would be paid the next day, spending it in twenty different ways. There would follow domestic details, some grumbling about the very high price of potatoes, or how long the winter was lasting, or the rising cost of fuel, a lively discussion on the subject of how much was owing to the baker. In the end the arguments got more and more bitter and each of them showed their character in picturesque language. As I listened to these people I could throw in my lot with them, feel their rags on my back, walk in their worn-out shoes. Their wishes, their needs, all entered my being, or mine theirs. It was like dreaming wide awake. I railed with them against the bosses who tyrannized them, or against the bad practices that forced them to go back again and again before they got paid for their work. Abandoning my own habits, becoming somebody else through the intoxication of my moral faculties, and playing this game whenever it took my fancy, that was my entertainment. To what do I owe this gift? Is it second sight? Is it one of those qualities that drive one towards madness if exercised too often? I've never gone into the reasons for this power. I have it and use it, and that's that. All you need to know is that, beginning then, I took apart the components of that heterogeneous mass we call the people and analysed them and could evaluate their good and bad qualities. I already knew how useful this area of Paris might be—this seedbed of revolutions with its heroes, inventors, practical scientists, rogues and villains, virtues and vices, all weighed down by poverty, choked by neediness, soaked in wine, worn down by strong liquor. Impossible to imagine how many affairs come to nought, how many forgotten dramas are played out in this sorrowing city. So many horrible and beautiful things! Imagination can never capture its secret truth, none will uncover it. You have to go too far down to dig out these wonderfully tragic or comic stories, masterpieces that chance engenders. I don't know how I have so long kept from you the story I am about to relate. It is one of those curious tales left in a sack and extracted on a whim by memory, like a lottery ticket. I have many, as singular as this one, also buried away. But their turn will come, you may depend upon it.

One day my cleaning-woman, the wife of a working man, came and asked if I would honour them with my presence at the wedding of one of her sisters. So that you should understand what kind of wedding this was, I ought to tell you that I used to give this poor woman forty sous a month to come every morning and make my bed, clean my shoes, brush my clothes, sweep the room, and prepare my lunch. The rest of the time she went to turn the crank of a machine and earned ten sous a day at this taxing job. Her husband, a cabinet-maker, earned four francs. But as there were three children in the family, he was scarcely able to afford to put bread on the table. I have never come across people more unswervingly honest than this man and woman. After I had left the area, Madame Vaillant, a woman who had never in her life managed to save a penny, came to wish me happy birthday every year for five years and bring me a bunch of flowers and some oranges. Poverty had brought us closer. I was never able to give her more than ten francs, which I had frequently borrowed from someone else, just for that purpose. Which explains my promise to go to the wedding; I was hoping to forget my cares in the happiness of these poor people.

The feasting and dancing all took place in a wine-seller's in Rue de Charenton, a large upstairs room lit by reflecting tin lamps, with grubby wallpaper up to the height of the tables and wooden benches around the walls. In this room eighty people, dressed in their best, flanked by bouquets and ribbons, all enlivened by the spirit of la Courtille, with flushed cheeks, were dancing as though there were no tomorrow. The bridal pair kissed, to the general satisfaction, and everyone shouted 'Ho ho!' and 'Ha Ha!' facetiously, but in truth it was much less indecent than the shy glances of well-brought-up young ladies. Everybody expressed an animal pleasure that was somehow very infectious.

But neither the faces in this gathering, nor the wedding, nor anything about this company has to do with my story. Just bear in mind how strange the setting was. Imagine the humble wine-shop with the red paint, smell the wine, listen to the merry shouts, and tarry awhile in this place, surrounded by these working people, these elderly men, these poor women wholly intent on enjoying their night out!

The orchestra consisted of three blind players from the Quinze-Vingts; the first played the fiddle, the second the clarinet, and the third the flute. All three were paid in total seven francs for the evening. At that price, naturally, they played neither Rossini nor Beethoven, they played whatever they wanted or were able to. Nobody made any adverse comment, tactfully! Their music was so hard on the eardrums that after I had cast my eyes over the assembled company, I looked at this blind trio and was disposed at once to be sympathetic towards them, as I recognized them for what they were by their dress. These musicians were in a window recess and you had to be right up close to make out their facial features. I didn't get near to them straight away. But when I did, why, I don't know, that was that, the wedding and the music disappeared, my curiosity was intensely aroused, and my whole being passed over into the body of the clarinet player. The fiddler and the flute-player both had common faces, instantly recognizable as those of the blind, strained, attentive, and

grave. But the clarinettist's face was one of those phe-
nomena that bring the artist and philosopher up with
a start.

Imagine a plaster head of Dante, lit by the red glow
of the oil-lamp and crowned by a thatch of silvery
white hair. The bitter and sorrowful expression in this
magnificent face was ennobled by blindness, for the
dead eyes came to life again through the force of his
thoughts. They seemed to burn, with a single unremit-
ting desire written plainly across his domed forehead,
criss-crossed by lines like the courses of an old wall.
This aged man was blowing into his instrument at
random, paying no attention whatsoever to the rhythm
or the tune, lowering or raising his fingers, moving the
old stops automatically, not caring what false notes he
made. The dancers took no more notice than did my
Italian's fellow musicians—for I was hoping he was an
Italian, and indeed he was. Something noble and despotic came together in this old Homer who contained
within him an *Odyssey* that was destined for oblivion.
He had a nobility so real it triumphed over his misery,
a despotism so defiant it towered above his poverty.
Not one of the violent passions that lead men to do
good as well as evil, make of them convicts or heroes,
was lacking in this nobly chiselled, pallid Italian
face, with overhanging, greying eyebrows casting their

shadows on to deep hollows in which one trembled to see the light of thought re-emerge, just as one fears to see brigands armed with flares and swords appear at the mouth of a cave. In this cage of flesh was a lion, a lion whose rage had exhausted itself uselessly against its iron bars. The fire of despair had burned itself out in its own ashes, the lava had cooled. But the furrows, the damage, traces of smoke attested to the violence of the eruption, the ravages of the fire. These thoughts, awakened in me by the look of this man, were as hot in my soul as they were cold on his face.

In between each *contredanse* the fiddle and the flute, who were seriously occupied with their glasses and bottles, would hang their instruments on the buttons of their reddish frock coats, reach out to a small table placed in the window recess where their drinks were, and hand the Italian a full glass, which he could not get himself, for the table was behind his chair; each time the clarinet nodded at them in friendly acknowledgement. Their movements were executed with the precision that always surprises one in the blind from the Quinze-Vingts, for they give the impression they can see. I got nearer to the three blind men to listen to their conversation; but when I was close they pricked up their ears, no doubt realizing I wasn't from the working classes, and fell silent.

'Where are you from, you playing the clarinet?'

'Venice,' replied the blind man, with a slight Italian accent.

'Were you born blind, or was it...?'

'An accident,' he answered quickly. 'Damned optic nerve.'

'Venice is a beautiful city, I've always dreamed of going there.'

The old man's face lit up, the lines in his face stirred, and he was moved to tears.

'If I went with you, you wouldn't be wasting your time,' he said.

'Don't talk to him about Venice,' said the violin, 'or our Doge will never stop; besides, the Prince has already got two bottles inside him!'

'Come on, let's play, Père Canard,' said the flute.

All three began to play. But when they set to playing the four *contredanses*, the Venetian could sense I was there, and he divined my all-consuming interest in him. His face no longer wore a cold, sad expression. I do not know what hopes animated his features, coursing like a blue flame through that lined face of his. He smiled, wiped his brow, that brow that was so bold and terrifying. And then he became as cheery as a man is when talking about the subject most dear to his heart.

'How old are you?' I asked him.

'Eighty-two!'

'How long have you been blind?'

'Nigh on fifty years,' he replied in a tone of voice that not only revealed his sorrow at losing his sight but also at being deprived of some important privilege.

'So why do they call you the Doge?' I enquired.

'Oh, for a joke,' he said. 'I am a patrician of Venice and should have been a Doge like anyone else.'

'What are you called then?'

'In these parts they call me *Old Canet*. My name has never been written any other way on the registers, but in Italian it is Marco Facino Cane, Prince of Varese.'

'What? Are you a descendant of the famous *condottiere* Facino Cane whose fortune passed to the dukes of Milan?'

'*E vero*,' he said. 'In those days, in order not to be killed by the Visconti, the son of Cane took refuge in Venice and had his name inscribed in the Livre d'Or. But the book no longer exists and nor does Cane.' And with a fearsome gesture he indicated both his defunct patriotism and his disgust for all humankind.

'But if you were a senator of Venice you must have been rich? How did you manage to lose all your money?'

At that question he raised his head as though he could see me, and with a truly tragic gesture, he answered, 'Misfortune!'

He no longer had a mind to drink; he waved away the glass of wine the old flute-player held out to him at that moment, and then lowered his head. These details were not of a kind to satisfy my curiosity. While the three instruments were playing the *contredanse*, I contemplated the old Venetian nobleman with all the emotion of a young man of twenty. In that wreck of a face I saw Venice and the Adriatic, I saw the city in ruins. I walked round this city held so dear by its inhabitants, I went from the Rialto to the Grand Canal, from the Esclavons quay to the Lido, I returned to the sublimely original cathedral. I looked at the windows of the Casa d'Oro, each ornamented in a different way. I beheld its ancient palaces rich in marble, in fact all the wonderful sights that seduce the educated man, the more so because he may paint them whatever colour he pleases and his dreams lose none of their poetry when faced with the real thing. I traced the career of this offspring of the greatest of the *condottieri*, seeking the origins of his unhappiness and the reasons for his profound physical and moral degradation, which rendered even more beautiful the sparks of nobility and greatness that the moment revived. We must have been thinking the same thoughts, for I believe blindness makes intellectual communication much swifter, since it prevents one's attention being distracted by external objects. The proof of our sympathy was not long coming. Facino Cane stopped playing, got up, came over and said: 'Let's go!' which produced in me something akin to an electric shock. I offered him my arm and we left.

When we were out in the street, he said: 'Will you take me to Venice, lead me there, do you have faith in me? You will be richer than the ten richest families in Amsterdam or London, richer than the Rothschilds, as rich as the *Thousand and One Nights*.'

I thought the man was mad, but in his voice there was a power that I obeyed. I allowed myself to be led along and, as though he were sighted, he led me to the old moat of the Bastille. He sat on a stone in a very quiet spot, where since that time they have built the bridge by which the Canal Saint-Martin connects with the Seine. I sat on another stone opposite this old man whose white hair shone like silver threads in the moonlight. The silence, scarcely disturbed by the rumbling which reached our ears from the boulevards, the purity of the night, everything conspired to make it a truly fantastic scene.

'You speak of millions to a young man and you really think he would hesitate to put up with a thousand ills in order to acquire them? Are you joking?'

'May I die unshriven,' he said passionately, 'if what I am going to tell you is not true. I was twenty, like you now; I was rich, I was handsome, I was noble, I began by committing the first folly, falling in love. I fell in love the way nobody does any more, to the point of hiding in a trunk and risking being stabbed, for nothing but the promise of a kiss. To die for *her* seemed to me worth my whole life. In 1760 I fell in love with one of the Vendramini, a girl of eighteen married to a Sagredo, one of the richest senators, a man of thirty, who was madly in love with his wife. My mistress and I were as innocent as two cherubs, but the *sposo* caught us talking about love. I was unarmed. His blow missed me, so I jumped on him and strangled him with my two hands, wringing his neck as you do a chicken. I wanted to go off with Bianca, she did not want to go with me. That's women for you! I left by myself, a marked man, my goods sequestered to the advantage of my inheritors. But I took my diamonds, five rolled-up paintings by Titian, and all my gold with me. I went to Milan, where nobody bothered me. The state was not in the least interested in my affair.

'One small observation before I carry on,' he said after a pause. 'Whether a woman's fancies have any influence or not on the child she is carrying, or at its conception, it is certain that when my mother was pregnant she had a passion for gold. I have a monomania for gold, and satisfying it is so necessary to my life that in all the situations I have found myself in I have never been without gold about my person. I am constantly handling gold. When I was young I always wore jewels and had two or three hundred ducats on me.'

So saying, he pulled two ducats from his pocket and showed them to me.

'I can smell gold. Though blind, I always stop outside jewellers' shops. This passion was my undoing, I became a gambler in order to play for gold. I wasn't a swindler, I was swindled. I was made bankrupt. When I had no more money I was consumed by the strong desire to see Bianca again. I went back to Venice secretly, I found her, I was happy for six months, hiding in her house and fed by her. I thought all my life would be lived in this delightful fashion. She was courted by the *provveditore*; he became my rival, Italians can sniff them out. He spied on us, surprised us in bed together, coward that he was! You can imagine how violent the fight was. I didn't kill him, but I did seriously wound him. This affair put paid to my happiness. From that day on I never again found a Bianca. I have experienced great pleasure; I have lived at the court of Louis XV amongst the most celebrated women; but never anywhere have I found the qualities, the grace, the love of my darling Venetian girl. The *provveditore* had his henchmen, he summoned them, the palace was surrounded and invaded. I fought, desiring to die in Bianca's presence, and she helped me kill the *provveditore*. Once this woman would not run away with me; but after six months of happiness she wanted to die with me, and she received several blows. They threw a big cloak over me, captured me, wrapped me in it, carried me to a gondola, and transported me to a dungeon in the wells. I was twenty-two, I held the handle of my sword so tightly that to get it they would have had to cut off my wrist. By a strange chance, or rather, thinking to make provision take precautionary measures, I hid this bit of steel in a corner in case it might be useful.

'They tended me. My wounds got better. None of them was mortal. At twenty-two you get over everything. They intended to behead me, I pretended to be ill to gain time. I thought I was in a dungeon near the canal, and my plan was to escape by making a hole through the wall and swimming across the canal, at the risk of drowning. These are the grounds on which

I based this hope: every time the jailer brought me my food I read the signs on the walls like: *To The Palace, To The Canal, To The Tunnel,* and in the end I understood the layout of the place, which was not a real concern to me but was explained by the unfinished state of the ducal palace at the time. Inspired by the desire to regain my freedom, I managed to make out, by feeling with my fingertips on the surface of a stone, an inscription in Arabic, in which the writer advised his successors that he had removed two stones from the bottom courses and dug out eleven feet of tunnel. In order to carry on his work you would have to spread the fragments of stone and mortar produced by the excavation over the floor of the dungeon itself. Even though the warders or inquisitors might have been confident that the structure of the building itself meant it only needed watching from the outside, the fact that the dungeons were reached down some steps made it possible to raise the level of the floor gradually without them noticing. This immense task had been in vain, at least for the unknown man who had undertaken it, for the fact that it had not been finished was evidence of his death. So that his dedication should not be forever wasted, it was necessary for a prisoner to know Arabic. But I had studied oriental languages in the Armenian convent. A sentence written behind the stone told of the fate of this poor man, a victim of his immense fortune, which Venice had coveted and seized.

'It took me a month to get any result. While I worked, and at the times when fatigue overwhelmed me I could hear the sound of gold, I saw gold in front of me, I was dazzled by diamonds. Oh, wait! One night my blunted steel hit wood. I sharpened the sword-stump and made a hole in that wood. In order to work I wriggled around on my belly like a snake. I stripped naked, holding my hands in front of me like a mole and using the stone itself to push against. At night, two days before I was due to appear before my judges, I made one last effort. I pierced the wood and my blade met nothing beyond. Imagine my surprise when I pressed my eyes to the hole! I had got through to the panelling of a cellar, where by a very pale light I was able to make out a pile of gold. The Doge and one of the Ten were in this cellar, I could hear their voices. From what they said I learned that this was the secret treasury of the Republic, the gifts of the Doges, and the reserves of the spoils called the 'Venetian denarii', that are levied on the traders' argosies. I was saved!

'When the jailer came, I suggested to him that he should help me escape and leave with me, taking all we could with us. There was no time to hesitate, and he agreed. A ship was setting sail for the Levant, all precautions were taken, Bianca aided the measures that I dictated to my accomplice. Bianca was to join us in Smyrna, not to arouse suspicion. In one night the hole was widened and we went down into the secret treasury of Venice. What a night! I saw four casks full of gold. Silver was piled up also in two heaps in the antechamber, leaving a way through the middle to cross the room, where the coins were banked up five feet high around the walls. I thought the jailer would go crazy. He sang, he jumped, he laughed, he leaped about in the gold. I threatened to strangle him if he wasted time or made a noise. In his delight he did not at first notice a table with diamonds. I threw myself upon them, to fill my sailor's jacket and the pockets of my trousers. By God, I did not even manage to take a third of what was there! Under the table were gold ingots. I persuaded my companion to fill as many sacks as we could carry with the gold, pointing out to him that that was the only way not to be betrayed to the authorities when abroad. "Pearls, jewels, and diamonds would give us away," I said to him. For all our greed we could only take two thousand pounds of gold, which necessitated six journeys across the prison to the gondola. The guard at the water-gate had been bribed with a sack of ten pounds of gold. As for the two gondoliers, they believed they were serving the Republic.

'We left at daylight. Out on the high seas, when I remembered that night, when I recalled the sensations I had experienced and saw that enormous treasury again where, according to my calculations, I had left thirty millions in silver and twenty millions in gold, several millions in diamonds, pearls, and rubies, I had the feeling I was going mad. I was mad for gold. We disembarked at Smyrna, and then immediately for France. As we went on board the French ship, God was good to me in getting rid of my accomplice. At the time I did not consider the deeper significance of this unfortunate turn of events, and I was very happy. We were so utterly wrought up that we were stupefied, not speaking to each other, and waiting to reach safety before we relaxed. It was not surprising that the rascal went off his head. You will see how God punished me.

'I only felt at peace again after selling two-thirds of my diamonds in London and Amsterdam, and exchanging my gold for coin on the open market. For five years I was in hiding in Madrid, and then, in 1770, I came to Paris under a Spanish name, and led a life of the greatest brilliance. Bianca was dead. In the middle of my life of pleasure, while enjoying a fortune of six millions, I was struck down by blindness. I do not doubt that this infirmity was the result of my period in the dungeon, my working at the stone, unless it was that my capacity for seeing gold harmed my visual powers and predestined me to lose my sight.

'At that time I loved a woman with whom I hoped to throw in my lot. I had told her the secret of my name, she belonged to a powerful family, and I had high hopes from the favours granted me by Louis XV. I had put my trust in this woman, who was the friend of Madame Du Barry; she advised me to consult a famous oculist in London. But after some months in that city I was abandoned by her in Hyde Park. She had robbed me of my fortune and left me destitute. I could not call upon anyone for help since I had to hide my identity which, if known, would deliver me over to vengeance in Venice; I was fearful of Venice. My disability was taken advantage of by people whom this woman had hired to spy on me.

'I won't go into all my adventures, they are worthy of Gil Blas. Your revolution arrived. I was forced to enter the Quinze-Vingts, to which this creature had me admitted after keeping me locked up in Bicêtre for two years like a madman. I never managed to kill her, I couldn't see at all, and I was too poor to hire someone to do it for me. If, before I had lost Benedetto Carpi, I had consulted him about the position of my dungeon, I would have known where the treasury lay and returned to Venice when the Republic was destroyed by Napoleon.

'Nevertheless, despite my blindness, let us go, you and I, to Venice! I will find the prison gate again, I shall see the gold through the walls, I shall smell it in the water where it's buried. For the events which have overthrown the power of Venice are such that the secret of this treasure must have died with Vendramino, the brother of Bianca, a Doge, who, I had hoped, would have made my peace with the Ten. I wrote notes to the First Consul, proposed a treaty with the Emperor of Austria, all of them sent me away as though I was mad! Come, let us leave for Venice, let us leave as beggars, for we shall return as millionaires. We will redeem my fortune, and you shall be my inheritor, you shall be Prince of Varese.'

I made no answer, for, seeing this white head and sitting in front of the stagnant black water of the moat of the Bastille, which resembled the canals of Venice, my head was whirling with all he had told me, which in my imagination was assuming the proportions of a poem. Facino Cane no doubt thought that I viewed him as everybody did, with pity and contempt, and made a gesture expressive of total despair. His narrative had perhaps taken him back to happier days in Venice. He seized his clarinet and played a melancholy

Venetian song, a barcarolle, for which he rediscovered his first talent, the talent of a nobleman in love. It was something like 'Super flumina Babylonis'. My eyes filled with tears. If a few late stragglers were walking along the boulevard Bourdon, no doubt they stopped to listen to this last prayer of the exile, the last regret of a name that was lost, in which was mingled the memory of Bianca. But soon gold took over again, and the fateful passion extinguished the light of youth.

'This treasury,' he declared, 'I can see it still, clearly as in a dream. I walk there, the diamonds sparkle, I am not so blind as you think. Gold and diamonds light up my night, the night of the last Facino Cane, for my title passes to the Memmi. Oh God! The murderer's punishment has begun early! *Ave Maria...*'

He recited a few prayers, which I couldn't hear.

'We shall go to Venice!' I cried when he got up.

'So have I found my man!' he cried, his face alight.

I took him back, giving him my arm. He shook my hand at the gate of the Qunze-Vingts, just as a few wedding-guests were returning home, shouting at the tops of their voices.

'Shall we go tomorrow?' asked the old man.

'As soon as we have the money.'

'But we can go on foot, I'll ask for alms... I am strong, and you feel young with the prospect of gold before you.'

Facino Cane died that winter, after being ill for two months. The poor man had taken a chill.

Paris, March 1836.

Rue des Larmes

Frédéric Fajardie

Paris, 25 February, 1972. 9 p.m.

He couldn't get over it.

He wondered if he was dreaming. But his feet, hitting the asphalt at every step, persuaded him of the opposite.

He thought perhaps it was an illusion and that he was actually dead, quite dead, spreadeagled on the pavement in Rue de Charonne.

But no: if he were dead, he wouldn't be thinking any more. The black, the enormous black hole of non-life, the darkness that absorbs and in which one is dissolved, the lacquered black of coffins and of the inquisitors' robes . . .

'It's only when I'm making love that I know I'm not dead,' he muttered.

He looked around wildly for a woman, any woman, but the narrow street was almost empty. And anyway, what was this street?

He looked up, and with difficulty made out the words: 'Rue de Lappe.'

Rue de Lappe. It sounded like a song. A folk song. Something to do with lilies of the valley. No, the people. No, the Communist party. Yes, Rue de Lappe, it was a song sung by some Party sympathizer or other. Jean Ferrat? No, older than that. Maurice Chevalier? No, he was the one who sucked up to the Nazis. Perhaps...Perhaps, yes, Francis Lemarque, the one who sang 'Marjolaine' and 'Bal, petit Bal'...

He was alive, more alive than he had ever been, and he loved this mysterious Rue de Lappe where everything gave him back life and hope...

He was dimly aware that he was staggering around, that his bumping into things wasn't normal, but he couldn't help it.

There was something wrong. Perhaps it was emotional: basically the day must have been appalling, dramatic, out of the ordinary...

Exhausted, he leaned against the window of number thirty-four, an old shop with the sign *Salaisons d'Auvergne* outside.

Briefly, he felt hungry. Then vomited at length, coughing and showering the shop window and the pavement.

Sick, his eyes running with tears, he went on his way uncertainly, but he was short of breath and again needed to lean against a shop-front.

He had the feeling that his brain, now with a will of its own, was parting company with him, and in order to reassert its command over it he raised his eyes to number thirty, muttering:

'Thirty. Thirty Rue de Lappe. Leather straps and rubber. SKF ball bearings. Thirty Rue de Lappe... Bee bearings, bearings of bees, noise of machine guns...'

At certain moments a rosy veil seemed to be thrown over people, buildings, and objects. A very pale pink, very pure, a foamy pink sublimate. He could see himself, a small boy again, accompanying his father recovering metal from factories that had been shut down. Mostly they were non-ferrous metals, copper for example: electric cables, big extinguishers... Everything was rapidly piled into the old van and, once they had reached home, his father sawed it all up, producing as he did so an extraordinary pink powder which formed a small conical mound under the vice.

'A dust that cuts to the quick!' he muttered. 'When childhood is brought up against matter, it's the end of the golden age.'

Opposite number twenty-seven, he raised his head and saw an old three-storey house with attic rooms set back.

A slum—a slum like the one he had grown up in. The same washing outside the windows, the same food-safe with a very fine mesh . . .

He thought he could make out a dead pigeon in the gutter on the roof, its wings modestly folded in upon the great black mystery.

What was there that was worse than death? Madness perhaps. Or absence.

Absence. Oh yes! Abdicate! Desert! Leave for the interior, come face to face with yourself: the horror!

He looked again at the corpse of the pigeon. He had always liked birds, including iron ones, when he did his military service on some godforsaken base in the airforce, on the border with the East, in snow and fog.

But it all seemed so far away!

The pink veil grew thicker, taking on the occasional tint of lilac. Blinding pains were shooting through his skull.

'Mustn't think any more. In my head the old and the new are hammering it out. They forget that it's me that pays!'

He had progressed a few metres and presently found himself in front of a wide shop-front painted pine green on which he read, in yellow letters: Semelys Makers of Metal Counters.

Semelys: what a strange name! Yet familiar. He pondered it, wiping the blood trickling from his ears on the back of his sleeve...

'Semelys... Semelys.'

Ah yes, now he remembered! He wasn't quite fit for the scrap-heap yet! Semelys, that reminded him of Semmelweis, a nineteenth-century doctor from Hungary who had been the first to advocate asepsis in childbirth. And Louis-Ferdinand Céline had dedicated his thesis to him, which was to say the very first thing he wrote.

Finding Semmelweis again in the Rue de Lappe was odd, all the same!

But he himself, what was he doing in the Rue de Lappe? And why were his nose and ears bleeding? And where had he come from? Did he have a house, a roof over his head? Or perhaps a little apartment?

Now he was lost. It was all quite simple: he didn't know where to go. A child, a baby...

Babies are like everyone else in spite of what it seems: death is tagged to their lives from the very day they are born.

He stopped in front of number twenty-two, a sort of depot, and tried to come to some decisions. First he resolved not to talk out loud any more. Next, to go back over what had happened in the course of the day. It ought to be possible. For a start, there had been the dawn, the whitening horizon, the presence of sunshine...

No, today the sun had put his dark glasses on. And yet, this scarlet veil... The scarlet and black... A novel, of course. And the anarchist-syndicalist colours.

YES!

There, everything was working again! He was a political militant! He belonged to the far left. He was a Maoist and his group was called the Cause of the People, formerly the Proletarian Left, now defunct.

How good to remember things again. It seemed to him that his strength was returning, and for a few metres he walked almost normally.

On his right he saw the Philippe Auguste passage, at the far end of which he thought he could make out a small factory. Unless it was a large shed.

Militant!

Of course! How could he have forgotten such an important thing!

He had just taken part in a demonstration. A demonstration intended to honour the memory of the eight people murdered at the Charonne metro on 8 February 1962: small chance of him forgetting the date because he was at that demonstration as well, when he was only a little boy, holding his father's hand.

He wondered at being able to recall all that in such detail.

So it was a an act of homage, as well as a protest against the discrimination suffered by immigrant workers in France.

Utterly worn out, he stopped in front of a very old café called Le Petit Café, but it was closed.

The smell of tear-gas floated in the air, irritating his throat and making his eyes smart.

'Rue de Lappe, Street of Tears,' he thought to himself.

He pulled up the collar of his leather jacket with a pro-Chinese badge on it, then, pushing his hands down into his pockets, to his surprise found some bolts.

Bolts?

He struggled to understand. Obviously the demo had been extremely violent, but why was it intended to be? After all, it wasn't one of those anti-fascist counter-demos directed against the little neo-nazis, was it?

He felt he was going to faint and sat down on the pavement with his feet in the gutter.

He could see the Balajo sign from where he was sitting.

He was surprised. He knew the name and what it meant, but he was disconcerted by the unlikely event of him being there outside this mythic venue.

'You okay?'

Somebody was speaking to him. To him.

He raised his eyes and saw an old man, shabby and unshaven, holding several plastic bags.

'You not well, friend?' the man said once more.

'I'm okay. I'll be all right now.'

The old man with the bags looked every bit the tramp, but so much concern was touching. He himself was nothing, nothing special, and all his life he had been extremely sensitive to any show of warmth.

'Do you ever get drunk, by any chance?' asked the tramp.

'No, I always drink water...'

'Oh, kind of sick, are you?'

'No. But alcohol, it makes you remote, dependent, and your enemy can take... Oh, it doesn't matter.'

He brought his sentence to an abrupt conclusion: What was the point in coming out with these maxims to this poor creature, who obviously spent his days not obeying them?

'You hungry, friend?'

'Yes ... hungry ...'

The tramp opened one of his bags marked 'Inno' and took out a small packet wrapped up in newspaper which he started to remove, saying:

'Here, have this. It's a Choco BN. They're good for you, Choco BN. Perhaps not as good as gingerbread, but all the same ... Oh, gingerbread with butter on! And what about lardy-cake! Even tastier, lardy-cake!'

'Not hungry now. ... thanks.'

The tramp shook his head disapprovingly and replied:

'You change your mind pretty quick!'

'I'm sorry.'

'Up to you. But I can tell you this Choco BN isn't more than a week old.'

'Thanks ... thanks very much, but I'm not hungry any more ...'

The tramp scratched his head reflectively saying:

'This area is full of cops, you know. Nasty ones in helmets. Be better for you to scarper. Don't forget, they're supposed to have killed some chap at Renault only just now. Go on, vamoose.'

He watched the tramp go off, cursing himself. How could he have forgotten that? Of course! Renault's own security guards had killed one of their own workers, a militant of the Proletarian Left called Pierre Overney. And that would explain the bolts, the violence, and the impossibility, more or less, of forming up in another group of more than 100 or 150 without the cops intervening immediately and charging at them.

At least he had escaped arrest.

He could imagine the usual account and the eternal reports by the cops in *Le Monde* under the heading 'Disturbances': 'The judiciary has opened an inquiry and is proceeding with it as a priority, deploying all possible means to shed light on this affair and bring the guilty to justice.'

Bad news for them.

On the contrary! It would credit them with a powerful infrastructure, implicate them in a fearful 'international conspiracy', them—'the enemy within'.

If only they knew! Oh, not the cops or the corrupt press, who were well aware of how few and ineffectual they were, but the great mass of the people, of whom they were supposed to represent the 'conscious and organized avant-garde'.

Obvious, however, that the leftist café would soon be pulling down its shutters!

How adrift they were!

He could well imagine those fools the Trotskyites trying as ever to draw something to their own advantage from a game they never played, all the party squabbles and all the sickening manoeuvrings of the little factions right next to the still-warm body of Overney.

Where was it, the spirit of May '68? Roaming round the battlements of Elsinore?

He resolved to think about something else and tried to get back on his feet.

The Rue de Lappe seemed to be never-ending, and for some strange reason he did not want to reach number one.

Yes, number one Rue de Lappe scared him silly. It was crazy, it was irrational but he couldn't help it.

May '68!

'You may try to burn your bridges,' he grumbled, 'but your mind builds them up again as soon as your back is turned.'

After that immense period of hope he ought not to have gone on living. May '68 was like the first time with a girl: it's not often as good as that again!

The idea pleased him. Better with a girl, that meant love with a big L. Better than May '68—it was the Revolution, the great red, unending festival.

He thought about the girl he had caught sight of in July '68 at the faculty of science in Jussieu . . . She was at the UJCML stand—a very hardline pro-Chinese group.

They had looked at each other . . . But what a look! What promise! He had not overcome his shyness but was so convinced he would see her again . . . A look that lasted thirty seconds, or maybe a minute . . . The only time in his life when he had given himself wordlessly to a girl who had likewise given herself to him. When all was said and done it would have been enough—today he was sure of it—to go and take her hand . . .

How beautiful she was! A fringe over her forehead, straight-cut hair, a mouth that was marvellously drawn, very lovely eyes, sad and a bit distant . . .

He had never seen her again.

Not one of the former members of UJCML remembered her. As for the agency photos—that day the whirring of the Nikon cameras almost constituted a background noise—those shitty photo agencies didn't let just anybody see their archives.

What had happened to her? What fool was she living with? How was she getting through life? With what hopes, what philosophy, what plans?

He had reached number six, an old delicatessen with marble counters.

At present he was no longer in any doubt, and so much happiness was swamping him, he almost felt sick with it: she was going to come!

She was going to come now, this very minute! There were thousands of streets in Paris, the most outlandish, the most beautiful, the most sordid, the most banal, the most surprising... There were thousands of names, for heaven's sake, all he had to do was snap his fingers to find a street in the south, another in the centre, and a third in the north! And little streets too!

He snapped his fingers, saying Rue du Banquier, Rue Quatrefages, Rue Armand-Carrel.

But she had nothing to do with those streets for the very good reason that she lived in the Rue de Lappe. Everything had therefore conspired to bring him here at this precise moment, to meet *her*.

Bloody old destiny, he muttered. You've taken your time bringing us together again!

He realized he had just fallen down, right there, in the middle of the road.

He was very scared. He remembered perfectly now. Every single detail: the Rue de Charonne drowned in clouds of tear-gas, the policeman on a bike coming from nowhere holding his heavy carbine by the barrel, the terrifying blow of the rifle-butt on his head, that crack, that first fall, and the voice of a policeman shouting:

'Shit, Jean-Pierre, you've killed him! Let's get out of here!'

He saw feet around him, people talking . . . He caught words, shreds of language:

'A doctor won't do! Better call an ambulance!'

'An ambulance and straight to hospital. I've seen a man in a road accident with blood spurting out of his ears like that: the guy was dead within half an hour, believe you me.'

He felt himself being lifted up.

He looked around wildly at the blurry film of faces surrounding him.

June 1987

I stopped that day.

Everything stopped. I broke down. Especially when the surgeons talked about 'lesions'. They weren't really in agreement about the word 'irreversible . . .'

So I never spoke again, I learned to drool, to keep a fixed stare for hours on end, absent, devoid of all expression.

My new plan is simple: when I have regained my self-confidence I shall go back to the Rue de Lappe. And this time it will be all right.

Probably *she* is there expecting me.

My previous plan was very badly worked out. Errors all along the line. That's it, the 'general line', as they say in the Organization. The general line was false. I thought I'd find her in this hospice in the Creuse where I am living now. Not as a patient, but I was certain she would have to go there to see a relative, friend or former neighbour... And there, *bien sûr*, she would have seen me.

I often imagine the dumbfounded expression she would have had on her face then: it's a long way from the faculty at Jussieu to this desperate hospice in the deepest Creuse!

In one sense it's a pity that didn't happen. Our story would have taken a different course, far far removed from all ordinary stories.

Well I was sure of doing the right thing but I made a mistake: never mind! As the English say: Never too late. No, never too late!

I'm going to see the boss, and although he looks to me like the worst kind of Trotskyist, I'll tell him: 'There, I'm fine. Just fine. I'm more or less cured. So comrade, you better give me an exit permit double-quick because I've got a very pressing meeting in the Rue de Lappe.'

What I don't have any more is any notion of time. I don't know if I've been trailing from hospital to hospice, from one province to another for days or weeks.

Or is it months?

So is it... let me see... 1973?

All the same, I should really get a grip now I'm better! Otherwise She might move out.

I'm not afraid of her forgetting me, that's impossible: after all, have I forgotten her? No, but I'm afraid of something going wrong again, of missing another rendezvous.

Yes, I'll tell them that, I'll say I am leaving on my 1973 summer holidays.

Or the autumn break... Or Christmas.

I'll do that as soon as I am better, as soon as I have got my confidence back.

Soon, very soon.

January–May1987

Story

Paul Fournel

Story 1

This is the story of a man who meets a woman and falls
in love with her. They meet in a nice little café, the sort
that may still be found in parts of Paris. One look and
he realizes she's the one, his Amélie. To him she is
lovely as the dawn, fresh as the dew, altogether a ray
of sunshine. He starts to court her in the time-
honoured way, with little presents. He buys her a
bouquet of flowers which she leaves on the café table.
He brings her sweets she will scarcely touch. An un-
happy-looking waiter brings them two glasses of sparkling wine that goes to their heads somewhat...

She plays hard to get, as is right and proper, then
allows him to kiss her under the dark archway of a large
house.

Mad with delight, he rushes into the block of flats where he lives, to tell the concierge about his good fortune, and to give her his parrot to look after while he goes away for a few days' holiday with his new lady-love.

They are on the Channel coast in pursuit of love. He squeezes her tight, tight in his arms till it wears her out, and she puts up with it with the occasional weary sigh which makes his eyes cloud over. He senses in her the weight of a mystery, the burden of a secret.

One evening, just as the sun is disappearing into the sea, she confesses she is the mother of a little boy who doesn't have a father and is being fostered. A tear rolls down her lovely cheek.

The man's heart gives a lurch: he is anxious to see the child immediately. She hesitates, is in two minds, weeps copiously. They leave.

They are in among some dingy miners' cottages. They hesitate for a long time between houses that all look exactly alike and then enter a squalid flat which is in semi-darkness. Everywhere is filth and disorder. A dishevelled woman is being hit by a drunk in front of a terrified small boy, too weak even to cry. The man is outraged. The mother rushes to take the child. The drunk places himself between them. If they want him to let the child go they must hand over a tidy sum of money. A fight ensues: the drunk threatens to hit the child with a poker. The harpy attacks the young mother and calls her names. The man throws himself into the fray, seizes the child, gets struck on the head by the poker, and turns the weapon on his aggressor.

The drunk is on the floor, pierced through the heart by the poker, his dishevelled widow on her knees next to him. The little boy is in his mother's arms; the man takes her hand and pulls her away. The three of them make good their escape.

They settle down to life in the man's flat. It's not easy, as the young woman doesn't get on very well with the concierge. Her little boy is allergic to the parrot and the concierge doesn't want to look after it any more. The child is often silent and withdrawn.

The man has frequent lapses of memory because of the poker blows on his head.

On the surface, however, life is calm and he is happy with his woman and her young son. He goes to work regularly until the night there comes a knock on the door. He opens it. Two detectives are on the landing.

Story 2

This is the story of a single mother who spends the worst part of her life in a sordid café on the outskirts of Paris. Whole days go by while she kills time with a small black coffee, gone cold, in front of her, wretchedly ogling the local drunks in order to make ends meet. She has abandoned her child to a couple of money-grabbing rogues who squeeze out of her the small amount of cash she has left. The child's father has vanished, and anyway she is not very sure who the father is. She had several to choose from.

One murky evening a man comes into the bar, leans on the counter, and suddenly catches sight of her. His face is transformed. She laughs inwardly at the effect she has on him.

He goes over to her shyly and starts to flirt with her, like an adolescent. He brings her flowers (she loathes flowers because they give her an allergy), he offers her sweets, which she refuses because she is slimming. He pays her compliments. He is soppy. She doesn't find him very attractive, and really he's not much fun to be with.

She allows him to kiss her under a nearby archway, not because she especially wants to, but because she can't be bothered to put up a fight. He hardly dares touch her. He suggests a couple of days at the seaside, and she agrees because she doesn't often get the chance to go off anywhere.

When they get to their small hotel he can't get enough of her, and she lets him have his way. She's used to it. The flowers in the garden and the newly mown grass bring tears to her eyes. She talks distractedly about her son, as she does with all her passing lovers, in the hope of tapping them for a few euros towards his board. The man is fired with enthusiasm and wants to go and fetch the child, come what may.

She tries to restrain his eagerness but it's no use. She wonders what she will do with this kid in Paris. Secretly she phones the wicked pair to tell them to prepare a rough reception if they want to hang on to their income.

They arrive at the cottage, the terrified kid is screaming, the villain brandishes his poker, the old woman tears her hair out. They overdo it a bit. The rogue bashes the man on the head and this great wimp is transformed into a fury. He seizes the poker and thrusts it straight into his paunch.

And off they go with the kid.

They settle down in Paris in the man's small apartment. There's no way they can keep his disgusting parrot. It has to stay with the horrible concierge's odious canary. The young woman leaves her child with the concierge as soon as the man's back is turned and goes back to her old haunts to earn a bit of pocket-money. When the waiter sees her come back his melancholy mug splits into a smile. In the paper she reads that the police have come to the conclusion that the poker murder was the settling of accounts between two drunks.

This conclusion doesn't suit her. How is she going to get rid of this chap, who is stuck on her and who is doing all he can to win her child's affections?

The weeks go by, and one blessed afternoon at the café she makes eyes at a man in an off-white mackintosh. She drags him under the next-door archway, and while he lifts her skirt he confides that he is a detective. 'I could tell you things that might interest you,' she says between sighs.

Story 3

This is the story of one of the last concierges in Paris. One of the few that haven't been replaced by a digital code. Faithful to her job in the lodge she sees everybody from her flats and from the neighbourhood go past. Scraps of people's lives float in and out: their comings and goings, tiny events which make up the jigsaw of her days. She rewrites the story of every one of them out of the bits and pieces life presents her with.

She complains each day about having to take up the letters, her legs being so bad. She grumbles about the noise on the stairs, she keeps an eye on the tradesmen delivering, she stops the ones whose faces are unfamiliar from going upstairs. She is disagreeable to the tenants who go to bed late and nice to the ones who appreciate her good qualities.

She shares her joys, her troubles, and her items of news with her canary who whistles in his cage outside the window of her lodge. You'd swear that bird understands everything!

Suddenly the calm little life of the man on the third floor seems to be turned upside down. He hums a tune as he climbs the stairs, he comes down holding a bouquet of flowers, a bag of sweets... The concierge is extremely excited because she can scent love a mile off. 'At last, someone in the flats has fallen in love,' she says to her canary, 'life will brighten up a bit now.'

The man in question has donned a lovely yellow tie. He no longer wears his old pullover. He wears a jacket now. 'His lady love must be rather posh!'

And then one morning he rushes into the lodge holding his parrot. 'Keep him for me please for a few days, it's a matter of love or death. He'll be company for your canary.'

She accepts the bird's perch in the name of romantic love, asks how to look after him, and watches her tenant disappear, humming a tune.

'Some people have all the luck,' she says to the parrot, who answers, 'Not much!' in such an unpleasant voice the canary puts her wings to her ears.

The block of flats returns to normal, until the night when the man comes back, dishevelled and clutching a little boy, trailing behind him a nondescript woman with a vacant stare. The concierge gives him his keys and asks him to take his parrot back up. Too late, he is already on the second floor.

The new tenant is a bad woman. The concierge doesn't take long to reach this conclusion. She won't take the parrot back, and as soon as the nice man has gone to work she disappears, abandoning the child in the lodge. The concierge doesn't make a fuss because the child always arrives with a big banknote and a sweet smile. You get fond of children like that.

She stands on the doorstep watching the woman leave. She'd give a lot to know where she goes to spend her days.

Early one morning two detectives arrive. They show her their badges and ask for the man's flat. A quarter of an hour later they come down again with the man and the lady. The kid comes down right behind them, crying, and slips into the lodge.

'And what am I supposed to do with the boy?' shouts the concierge on the doorstep as she watches the van leave.

'Not much!' answers the parrot.

Story 4

This is the story of a canary that lives and sings in a concierge's lodge in a district in Paris, a canary typical of that temperate zone, living in a cage 50 × 30 × 30. A concierge's canary with an embroidered cover on its cage.

His days pass by and all seem much the same, from the outside at least: a breakfast of seeds, fresh water, a chat with the concierge as she leans over her coffee. The first contact with the pigeon network and the sparrow network. News of the passages expected that day: a V of storks going South, a V of greylag geese. A family of magpies is feared to be definitely settling above the next door block of flats. Apart from that, nothing special to report about the black crow, the titmouse, the chiffchaff, and the bunting, all the usual gang.

While the concierge is on the stairs, the canary does his beak on his cuttlefish bone, the most precious of his tools. He works at the shape, the sharpness, the point-edness. He makes it into a perfect trumpet-shape which allows him to send out his inimitable warble that goes right through the walls, pierces the window-panes, and rises up to the pinnacle of the land of birds. His freedom.

The big event of his life is the arrival of 'Not much!' the parrot. One day the man from the third floor hurtles in with this monster and sticks it right there next to his cage. It's just too much. The odious animal is free on his perch, with one small chain attached to his claw. He is green and red, a real bruiser. He looks stupid. When he pulls on his chain to the maximum length, he can reach the canary's seed tray; the canary can't stand it. Stupid and thieving.

It needs to be said that parrots do not speak bird language and therefore live in an intermediate world, a world where they misunderstand others and are themselves misunderstood.

The atmosphere in the lodge gets sticky.

The canary activates the whole of his network to track down the parrot's owner and bring him back at top speed. Some seagulls report that he is at the seaside. They relieve themselves on his hat. An owl says he is in the north, and takes up position on the windowsill of a miner's cottage. What he sees fills him with horror and he flies off into the night, screeching like an eagle.

The man returns with a woman and boy. The canary has a brief moment of hope. But, alas, they don't take the monstrous 'Not much!' back.

Battles ensue, during which, in spite of the concierge's valiant attempts, the parrot remains.

The swallow network, which is in direct contact with the police, warns the canary that trouble's brewing for the monsieur on the third floor. Big trouble. What do they do with parrots when someone gets put in gaol? Are they subject to the same punishment as their masters? 'Not much!' he screams stupidly.

The canary goes through a period of intense stress, during which they fear for his life. He loses his desire to sing, his feathers fade and spiral down to the bottom of his cage ... Who will rescue him from this sorry plight? The little boy! Abandoned by one and all in the lodge, he never stops whining: 'When's my mummy coming back? In a month? In a year?' And the parrot's answer is always the same: 'Not much!' Exasperated, the boy lands him a straight right-hander which shuts him up for good. The canary is left in peace and quiet, with his voice and his beautiful yellow feathers.

Story 5

This is the story of a little boy, father unknown, whose mother and stepfather have been thrown into prison for tearing him from the clutches of a couple of torturers who were fostering him. The boy, who witnessed the whole fight and saw the poker sticking in the villain's heart, was born under a sign of conflict. He is stubborn, obstinate, a real brute of a child.

On the day of their arrest his mother and stepfather abandon him with the concierge in the flats, a horrible fat slut with a half-bald canary.

When he asks when his Mummy is coming back, it's only the parrot who answers with a stupid 'Not much!' With an immediate straight right-hander, he sends the parrot to meet his ancestors. There is a short silence. The canary starts singing again. The child falls down on his knees in front of the green corpse, puts his head in his hands, and decides on the spur of the moment to be a good boy.

We meet him again some weeks later. He has asked permission from Mamie-Concierge to go and meet his mother when she comes out of prison. His mother, thanks to a secret agreement with the police, is released after being held for only a few weeks. There on the pavement he embraces her, and so tightly she has to break free from his clasp. He asks for news of his almost-father and promises to write to him faithfully every week. His mother is relieved that the parrot won't be there when she returns home.

We meet the boy again some years later. He has grown into a fine young man, radiating goodwill. He holds his mother's hand on the pavement opposite the entrance to the La Santé prison. The big day has arrived. His almost-father is being let out. His mum is in a mood but he knows it won't last long.

The family is sitting around the table and the boy tells how his two childhood torturers would send him for coal every day at the back of the cellar black as a stove, even though the apartment was heated by gas and had been for quite some time ... In spite of this he went back to the cottage during his holidays and had an emotional reunion with the woman who had tortured him. She had become good and gentle and, moreover, she is standing respectfully outside the front door along with her friend Mamie-Concierge and now would be the perfect time to invite them in for a big family get-together.

A few months later he has just received his Certificate of Excellence and is on his way home, whistling. As he goes past, Mamie-Concierge gives him a letter which has come for him. He goes up and opens it carefully on the kitchen table. Inside there is a sheet of paper with letters cut out of a newspaper; there's no indication who has sent it and it's unsigned. 'Suppose it was your mother who betrayed your stepfather to the cops? I've got proof.'

He puts his head in his hands. Is his mother a whore? Should he avenge his stepfather? Must he save his mother at all costs? Should he unmask the poison-pen writer? What is the right thing to do, what would be the greater evil? His head is in a whirl.

Story 6

This is the story of an unhappy waiter in a squalid little Paris bistro. A waiter without any life-history, and without any life, as so many of them are. A dreary tale. A waiter who dries the glasses at the back of a café and who has nothing to do but dream. He knows he's the last of his kind, the last wearer of the black apron, and that he will go to his grave from this seedy joint frequented by old men who play boules and will be snuffed out by the next gust of wind. He cherishes a passion for the clouds that float past in succession above the Sacré-Coeur and describes them at length in boring detail that drives him ever deeper into melancholia. Stratus, cumulo-nimbus, cirrus, they all float past, slowly.

The one bright spark in his life is the lady who comes to spend much of her day there. She arrives quietly like a little mouse and always sits in the same place. In his eyes she is the most beautiful woman in the world, and for that reason he never manages to utter a word to her. He has tried to describe to her a thousand times what a prime cumulus is like, to induce her to move next to the window, but it's all in vain. She remains forever the distant beloved.

When he calls out the ritualistic: 'Another one, Madame?' intending some sexual suggestion, it is in vain; nothing comes of it. She doesn't notice him.

On the other hand, she keeps a watchful eye on everyone else. And leaves nothing to chance. An opportunistic prostitute. Each time she disappears he rushes to the back door to watch the moment when she starts getting groped under the archway. Every time a dagger goes through his heart.

He can't even suggest they have that kind of love. They both deserve better. He writes her passionate letters that he doesn't sign. He unleashes torrents of love, floods of desire, storms of passion on to her. All in vain.

His life drags along in dreary sentimentality, with no movement forward or back. So he listens, makes enquiries, tries to find out everything he can about her. He reads the newspapers, the scandals, the miscellaneous items, the murders. He talks to the police who come by. He invents, embellishes, pretends to tell the truth. He knows now, from reliable sources, that she has had a son and abandoned him. He has guessed that the chap who didn't dare touch her in the doorway was crazy about her. The concierge, when she came for her coffee, told him they had gone off to the seaside. He has followed the mining-district story. He knows how the poker went straight through the man's cold heart. He knows how dreadful unhappy love affairs are. He knows who was holding the poker. When he reads the clouds he sees the pathetic face of the child. He knows the man in the raincoat who put his hand up the girl's skirt is a detective. He knows it's all too much for him.

He knows the evening has come. He cuts out the letters from the newspaper, sticks them on the blank sheet of paper, sticks the stamp on the envelope, throws the envelope in the postbox. He feels like the most poisonous poison-pen writer there ever was, and gulps down the whole beakerful of phenobarbitone.

Story 7

This is the story of a bunch of flowers left on a small café table in a popular district in Paris. A little bouquet like the ones sold by vendors on the street corner. Pansies, violets, sweet peas. A bouquet offered during the first flush of love, a bouquet put down and left there because of an urgent need to embrace.

A bunch of flowers picked up by the unhappy waiter and put without thinking in a glass on the counter.

A bunch of flowers stolen by the child from the counter when he comes to tear his father away from his last glass of pastis. A bunch of flowers whose water drips through the child's fingers on his way home ...

A bunch of flowers which momentarily brightens his mother's face before the long face of the drunkard father framed in the doorway makes her feel depressed again. A bouquet the mother throws into the yard next morning after the child has left for school, because she is allergic to flowers and anyway has more than enough reasons to be sad in her life.

A bunch of flowers the concierge picks up again to throw in the bin while grumbling about the untidiness of the tenants.

A bunch of flowers she puts on the lodge table for the time being because the postman arrives at that minute with the post. A bunch she picks up again a moment later and shoves briefly under her nose.

'It stinks,' she says to her canary.

A bouquet drying upside down in the concierge's lodge above the canary's cage.

A bouquet that turns round and round as it is drying.

A bouquet of dried flowers which has been placed by a good and generous young man on his mother's grave, just before his arrest.

The woman he has killed.

There or Elsewhere

Martine Delerm

Rue Mouffetard, perhaps.

You are having dinner in an Asian restaurant, with a décor of blood and gold. Rainbow-coloured fish come and stick their monstrous mouths up against the magnifying sides of the fish tank. The steamed ravioli *will* keep eluding your chopsticks. Friends are supposed to be meeting you to go to the cinema. You keep a look-out for them through the window.

Inside, the scents of rice, students laughing, candles. Outside, December. It's dark and the creeping rain is icing over the pavements. The trees on the Contrescarpe they have powdered white, they have planted two or three fir trees laced with garlands.

Around the square, the terraces of the cafés are noisy with music and voices behind their translucent curtains. Butane heaters, stiff as servants in Imperial China, mist the transparent plastic.

In the centre of the square, with the chain around the flower-bed for a pillow, a man, half-lying, shelters under a narrow umbrella. Police are bent over him. He shakes his head. He doesn't want to go. He doesn't need them. He's fine where he is. This patch of drenched asphalt is what he likes. The rain, the cold, that suits him. Why don't they bloody well leave him alone!

Your friends are late. They're on their way! Mobiles are handy, they let you warn others that you're not there yet ... For the beef with onions, you don't even bother using chopsticks. Against your shoulder the pane of glass is icy-cold. It must be freezing outside. You shiver. These electric radiators are not really adequate for a room this size ... Immediately you are sorry you had that thought. You are ashamed of yourself.

The police have gone. The man is alone, head under his umbrella, body on a sodden newspaper ... That's still what he would rather have. On the ground, far away from the dazzle of Christmas lights, you can't quite see him but you know he's there. From time to time a car goes round and lights him up for a moment in its headlamps. Brutally.

You can do nothing for him. You are behind the window. Glass or plastic, windows are made for this purpose. To keep people apart. Transparent walls have risen up between him and you, and they are insurmountable.

After the crystallized ginger, before you meet up with your friends who will join you directly at the cinema, you'll perhaps go and talk to him...That's what they say on television, you must have the courage to do that...you mustn't be afraid to go and speak to them...that's what they need...or else smile at them. Just smile at them...Smile, give him something. The change from the restaurant, or more...

He will grunt his thanks vaguely, move his lips a little. Like that, just to be friendly.

You'll go. You can do nothing else now. You will only help yourself, salve your own conscience. His misery is elsewhere. Out of reach. Always one remains behind the glass.

Saint Genevieve

Jacques de Voragine

The blessed Genevieve was born of good parentage. Her father was called Sévère, her mother Géroncie, and she came into the world in Nanterre, a village near Paris. One day the blessed Germain, bishop of Auxerre, went to the church in that village to pray and a great crowd gathered round him, Genevieve among them. Seeing her, Saint Germain, obeying divine inspiration, had her brought to him, and announced to the people around him that God had chosen her to be His Bride. He said that at her birth the angels had sung hymns of joy, and he celebrated the good fortune of her parents in having such a daughter, and proclaimed that the example of her virtue would persuade many sinners to turn away from their sinful ways. When she had approached him and he had insisted on her obligation to preserve her virginity in view of her becoming the bride of the Celestial Husband, she replied that that had ever been her dearest wish. And Saint Germain said to her: 'Take courage, daughter, act boldly, and try to prove by your works what you believe in your heart and profess with your lips. The Lord will sustain you and give you strength.' The next day he asked that Genevieve be brought to him again, and said: 'Listen, Genevieve, my daughter, remember you promised yesterday to preserve your body from all uncleanliness.' And she replied: 'I remember, Father.' Then the bishop picked up a bronze coin which was on the ground at his feet, according to God's wish, and on which was imprinted the sign of the cross, and said to Genevieve: 'Wear this always around your neck in remembrance of me and never allow any ornament made of precious metal or rich with pearls upon your neck or fingers.' And, planting a kiss upon her forehead, he bade her farewell and left.

One day, when there was a solemn feast, Genevieve's mother wanted to go to church, on the understanding that her daughter would stay at home. But as her daughter complained about this, she flew into a rage and slapped her. And immediately her mother was blinded. For two years divine punishment was visited upon her and she remained deprived of sight. But after that time her daughter's prayers obtained a cure for her.

Another time Genevieve was with some nuns who were older than her, and who were walking ahead of her, and they met the bishop of Chartres. And the prelate said that the one who was walking at the back should walk at the front, because she was full of celestial holiness.

Having lost her parents, she went to stay in Paris, and fell so gravely ill that she remained for three days without any sign of life, and her limbs were like those of a dead woman. But when she had recovered her health, she said that an angel had shown her the glory of the saints and the torments of the wicked.

When Attila, king of the Huns was threatening Paris and was on the point of taking it, most of the inhabitants, seized with fright, escaped to other towns where they thought they would be less exposed to danger, but Genevieve committed herself to unceasing watching and praying. And she reassured the citizens, telling them not to be unnecessarily alarmed and prophesied that the city would not be taken. But some citizens began to murmur, saying that her predictions were only a sham, and they plotted together to kill her. But an archdeacon of Auxerre arrived, saying: 'Be very careful not to commit such a crime, for our bishop, the blessed Germain, has always praised this young girl to the utmost and has announced that from her birth, God has chosen her to be His Bride.' And these wayward men renounced their wicked plan and the Huns withdrew.

A woman came to Paris from Bourges who, having become a nun, had been raped, and she wanted to speak to Genevieve. The saint asked her if she was a nun or a widow, and this woman replied that she had been raped by a man when she was a virgin and she told her at what time and in what place. And soon, overcome with shame, she beseeched Saint Genevieve to grant her forgiveness.

A four-year-old child chanced to fall into a well, and after three hours they got him out, lifeless. His mother, desperate and tearing her hair, carried him to Saint Genevieve, who began to pray for the child and spread her cloak over him, and immediately he was restored to life.

The city of Paris suffered famine after a long siege, and Genevieve, moved with compassion, boarded a ship and sailed down the Seine to get some provisions. Arriving at the place where there was a tree jutting out of the river and which often caused ships to founder, she addressed her prayers to the Lord and ordered the tree to fall, which it straightaway did, and two monsters were seen fleeing from it. And from that time on no ship has perished in that passage which sailors had so greatly feared before. When the virgin returned she distributed bread to the poor according to their needs.

One day she went to the city of Troyes, and a great crowd ran ahead of her, and they brought her a multitude of the sick of every age and of both sexes, afflicted by infirmities of all kinds. Amongst them there was a man who, having worked on Sunday, had been struck blind by divine punishment, and a young girl who had been blind for twelve years. Genevieve restored their sight immediately and sent them away praising God.

A young girl from the town of Meaux had been promised in marriage, but moved by Genevieve's example, she wanted to emulate her virtues and asked if she might be received into the company of nuns. The young man, filled with fury, pursued his betrothed and Genevieve had her enter a church nearby, whose doors closed miraculously, and she kept her thus from the anger of this furious man.

In Orleans Genevieve asked the father of a family to pardon a slave who had been guilty of a crime, and the father refused. When he went home he was gripped by a bad fever and only recovered his health when he agreed to the pardon the saint was asking.

On entering the church of Saint Martin in Tours, the saint delivered a large number of those possessed by devils, as soon as they were rubbed with oil. And when the vessel containing the oil was empty and there were still people possessed of the devil, the saint lay down clasping the vessel and immediately it was refilled with oil, which was used to cure a large number.

As to the abstinence of the saint and her other virtues, Vincent de Beauvais expresses himself thus in his *Miroir*: 'From her fifteenth year until she reached the age of fifty, she ate only barley bread and beans, and she boiled enough in a pot to last two or three weeks. She fasted five times a week, and always abstained from wine or anything which could provoke drunkenness. When she had reached fifty, obeying the advice of some bishops, she began to eat fish and take milk with her barley bread. She was utterly devoted to Saint Denis and to the place where he suffered martyrdom, and she wanted to build a church in his honour. She advised priests to contribute as much as they could towards this holy edifice and they replied: "We shall act to the utmost of our ability, but there is no lime at all here." And the saint replied: "Go to the bridge in your town and come back and tell me what you hear." They went and heard two swineherds saying to one another: "When I was busy looking after the animals entrusted

to me, I found a lime-kiln of an astonishing size."—
"And I found in the forest, under the roots of a tree that
the wind had brought down, a pile of lime which
I think has never been touched." When the priests
heard that, they came back giving thanks to God.
And when the saint heard about it, she shed tears of
joy. She charged the priest Génésius to oversee the
building of this church, and with all the townspeople
who hurried to help it was promptly erected. One day
the supply of drink for the carpenters failed and the
saint, having addressed a prayer to God, made the sign
of the cross on the jug and it was immediately filled to
the brim. One Sunday Genevieve went out before day-
break to go to the church of Saint Denis and the
lantern that was being carried in front of her was
snuffed out. The virgins who were accompanying her
were terrified because it was dark, so Genevieve took
hold of the lantern and immediately it lighted itself
again. And similarly, another time when she got up
after praying for a long time prostrate on the floor, a
candle she was holding flared up suddenly and some
who were sick took up in faith some pieces of the
candle and were cured.

'A woman stole the saint's shoes and when she got
home she lost her eyesight. She had herself led to
Genevieve, and throwing herself at her feet, she

confessed her sin and the virgin restored her sight by making the sign of the cross upon her eyes. Childéric, the French king, had a great deal of respect for her, and one day, fearing the saint would free some prisoners that he was intending to have killed, on entering Paris he ordered the gates to be locked. When she learned of this, the saint immediately hurried to set these poor people free. When she touched the gates they opened by themselves and she obtained from the king that the prisoners' heads would not be cut off. At this time the blessed Simon the Stylite was alive, who had forced himself never to descend from the top of a column. And they say that the rumours of Saint Genevieve's virtue had reached him and he conveyed to her the profound veneration in which he held her and asked her to remember him in his prayers. One day some who were possessed by devils were brought to her in the church of Saint Denis, and they were filled with extreme frenzy and screamed dreadfully. And she cured these poor people, and when their demons were expelled everyone present smelled a dreadful smell. From Epiphany to the end of Lent the blessed Genevieve shut herself away in her cell and had communication with no one but God, and gave herself up to ceaseless prayer. A young nun, curious to see what the saint did when she was on her own, was punished by becoming suddenly blind. But after Easter Genevieve came out of her cell and cured her by making the sign of the cross, after having addressed a prayer to the Lord. One day as she was praying in the church of Saint Martin, one of the cantors present at Divine Service was seized by the devil and began to tear himself. Saint Genevieve ordered the devil to go away, but as it was threatening to come out via the eye of the man possessed, the saint compelled it to come out through the vilest part of the body, leaving disgusting traces. Once when she was overseeing the harvest in her fields, the workers were at the point of being interrupted in their labours by a violent storm. But the saint said a prayer and not a drop of rain fell either on them or on what they had harvested, whereas heavy rain flooded all the places round about. She lived eighty years and her feast day is celebrated on the third of the calends of January.'

This is what Vincent de Beauvais tells us. And we add a few facts taken from documents that are very authentic and able to be trusted, conserved in the church dedicated to the saint. After her death a lamp placed on her tomb burned uninterruptedly, without there being any need to replenish the oil, and the sick who rubbed themselves with this miraculous oil were cured of their complaints. A deaf-and-blind man approached the tomb of the saint and recovered his sight and speech. A woman was advised in a vision to bring her son, who had been blind from birth, to this same tomb, and his eyes opened at the very moment of the mass when they were reciting the gospel story in which Our Lord miraculously restores the sight of the man who had been blind from birth. A man born dumb also had a vision which enjoined him to visit the saint's tomb, and he immediately spoke and gave praise to God. When the abbot then asked him what he was going to do, he answered that he didn't want to return home or leave that place and that he was resolved to dedicate his life to the service of Saint Genevieve. And the abbot, full of joy, bestowed a kiss upon him and gave him what he needed to subsist.

A robber escaped one day from prison as a result of the negligence of his warder and fled to the saint's sepulchre, and threw his arms around it, imploring the help of the blessed Genevieve. The warder pursued him and tried to tear him from this sanctuary, and in his anger he blasphemed against the saint. At once he fell to the ground and expired miserably and the robber was delivered.

At another time the river Seine increased immeasurably and flooded the Chapel of the Virgins that the saint had had built near the church of Saint-Jean-Baptiste. And when the waters had gone down it was discovered they had not touched the bed where Genevieve had died and which was preserved in that same chapel. When the Normans burned that edifice the body of the saint was transported to safety and continued to effect dazzling miracles. And when peace was restored again it was placed with the greatest of honour above the altar where it lies to this day.

Later, by divine punishment, a sickness which the doctors called *sacred fire* came to consume the limbs of men who used them for unjust purposes, and in the middle of the general desolation a holy priest from Paris named Étienne remembered that the blessed Genevieve had previously delivered the town under her protection from many and serious perils, and with the permission of the priest and the commune processions were instituted in which the body of the saint was carried in ceremony to the Cathedral of Notre Dame. And when the procession took place, as soon as the coffin entered the church, all those who touched it were cured, with the exception of three. The following year Pope Innocent visited the Gauls and, learning of the great miracle, rendered thanks to God and to the blessed Genevieve, and desired that each year a special celebration feast should be held to commemorate it. For some years this feast took place with all due solemnity, and once it happened that, through the fault of the canon who was afraid to spend too much money on it, it took place without the ornaments and number of candles that they normally used. And the next day, when the canon went in to the church, he fell down and died miserably without being able to utter a single word. And that was a sign to show with what veneration it was necessary to celebrate the saint's feast.

A great number of sick have been cured through touching the hem of her garments. And it is right to feel the utmost devotion to this blessed virgin, who prays ceaselessly for the people who venerate her, and for all Christianity, and who constantly answers the prayers of those who call upon her in perfect faith.

Expomodigliani. com

Martine Delerm

An eerie light hangs over the city. Dirty snow, frozen on the underside of the gutters, scars roof metal. The moonlight filters through the tall windows of the studio, and sheds a sickly pool of blue over the floor. An eye without an iris. On the unlit stove water has frozen in the bottom of a basin.

A young woman, not much more than a girl, is tirelessly repeating words about living to a body that is dying. Amedeo. Amedeo. But the man cannot hear them. She has been nursing him in her arms for hours. Her murmurs are weaving the very last thread of one soul to another. He is burning, trembling. He is remote. His rasping, weak intake of breath tears her apart. She does not want to know, but she does know. From the beginning, she has always known.

The Colarossi Academy, his painter's dreams, the escape to Nice, his daughter's smile...Shreds of the past surface, in any order, uselessly. The draught through the joins in the windows makes the smell of the linseed oil, damp cloths, and the walls coated with saltpetre worse. She holds him. Against her. She holds him tight.

They should have had...coal, money, Italian sunshine...but Zborowski is selling nothing, paintings are piling up, life is running out. He coughs. Jeanne's hair flames in the half-light. Her eyes are nothing more than the watery moonlight in which the silence that will follow is already being diluted. Emptiness, endless hours, the impossibility of living through them without him, without his voice, without his hands, without watching him paint. She is nursing him in her arms. Star-shaped blood stains the wooden floor. She wants day to break, the dark to be over.

Amedeo! Voices, steps on the stairs, fists on the door. Let them knock. What have they ever done for him? He is hers alone. She will not open the door. It is snowing.

It is snowing. It's 24 January, as before. Cloudy and grey over the city. Icy-cold. They are there, lined up over a hundred metres, resigned. They chat valiantly as they stamp their feet. A man coming back from work shivers, is amazed: you must be brave to queue in a cold like this! Why so many? Are there really so many people who enjoy that sort of thing?

It's snowing, like before. Musée du Luxembourg. Modigliani. The Angel with the solemn face. 23 October–2 March. www.expomodigliani.com. The queue edges slowly forward. To pass the time conversations are begun, phrases, words that are warming:

'I wouldn't have imagined in this weather...'

'But those women without any eyes are fascinating...'

'Yes, it's interesting...'

'Just what I was going to say!'

'He died young.'

'It was something awful, syphilis, I think...'

'I thought it was tuberculosis.'

'Yes, perhaps, a disease of his time.'

'But all the same, what a gift!'

'I find them all rather similar, don't you?'

'That's the *style*! That's what's called style: you either like it or you don't. Not something you can talk about. Seems lots of people do like it.'

'It's a good thing there are still people...'

It is snowing. Daylight is scarcely visible through the curtain of snowflakes that the wind is flattening against the glass. The door with the broken handle rattles ceaselessly. They have come and carried him away, they have said words of hope she has not heard. Now that their shouts have quietened in the absolute silence of his absence, Jeanne looks at, without seeing, the frames of canvases turned to the wall. Alone.

She is alone. The baby kicks in her belly. He moves, he is saying he wants to be born, that he's had enough darkness, that he is thirsting for colours, that he wants to know. The child moves but Jeanne does not feel him. The child is knocking but Jeanne does not hear him. She sits, her head a little on one side, her eyes vacant, her hands together on her lap, for ever immobile.

It is snowing. The queue is progressing towards the front of the museum. Under the velvet dais protecting the steps hang life-size photos. Amedeo Modigliani. Jeanne Hébuterne. So young. So beautiful. So alive. The two friends on their culture spree are open-mouthed before them:

'Just think, we have artists like that and we don't realize it!'

'It's often the way...I read somewhere that Picasso had painted one of his canvases over a picture by Modigliani...Even among themselves...'

'But at the same time it's good to suffer, suffering's necessary... Today they are over-protected, they don't produce anything worthwhile any more.'

26 January. It has stopped snowing. Paris is sleeping beneath a heavy thick sky. In the Rue Amyot, not far from the Luxembourg, it is three in the morning. A window opens on the fifth floor. A young woman falls. No one will know if she hesitated. Was she bare-foot as she crossed the room? Did she hear the regular breathing of those asleep? Did she kiss her daughter's forehead or just walk along the corridor? Sleepwalking. We shall know nothing of her fear or pain.

Only a woman, a painter of twenty-three. A painter we shall never go and see in an exhibition.

Minuet

for Paul Bourget

Guy de Maupassant

Terrible disasters hardly affect me at all, said Jean Bridelle, a bachelor of a somewhat sceptical bent. I've seen war at very close quarters: I have stepped over corpses without flinching. The harshness of nature or man may make us cry out in horror or indignation, but it does not tug at our heartstrings, or make a shiver run down our spines as does the sight of things of less moment.

Surely the worst pain we can experience is the loss of a child for a mother or the loss of a mother for a man; it is a violent, dreadful thing; it turns our world upside down, it tears us apart. Yet we get over these disasters just as we heal from an open, bloody wound.

But certain people we meet, certain things we glimpse or only guess at, certain secret sorrows, certain cruel tricks of fate that stir up in us a multitude of painful thoughts and open the mysterious door to moral suffering, complicated, incurable; all the deeper for seeming benign, all the more wounding for seeming unintelligible, all the more lasting for seeming factitious—such things leave behind a lingering sense of sadness, a bitter aftertaste, a feeling of disappointment which we shall be a long time getting rid of.

I have constantly in my mind's eye two or three things that others may well not have noticed, but which entered me as incurably as the long, thin sting of an insect.

You would perhaps not understand why I was so disturbed, and so lastingly, by these rapid impressions—or why they stayed with me so long. I shall tell you about just one of them. It dates from way back, but is as vivid to me as if it were yesterday. Though it may be that my imagination has run away with my emotions.

I am fifty now. I was young then, and studying law. Of a rather sad, dreamy disposition, steeped in a melancholic philosophy, I did not care for noisy cafés, rowdy friends, or stupid girls. I rose early, and one of my very favourite treats was to go for a solitary walk at about eight in the morning in the Luxembourg nursery gardens.

You never knew this place? It was like a forgotten garden from the last century, a pretty garden as pretty as the sweet smile of an old lady. Thick hedges separated the narrow, regular paths, quiet paths running between two assiduously pruned walls of foliage. The gardener's large shears never ceased aligning these dividing hedges; and here and there one came across flower-beds, borders of small trees lined up like schoolboys on an outing, companies of magnificent rose bushes or regiments of fruit trees.

One whole area of this charming little grove was inhabited by bees. Their straw hives, cleverly spaced on planks of wood, opened to the sunshine their doors no bigger than thimbles; and all along the paths you came across golden, buzzing bees, the true mistresses of this peaceful place, the real visitors to these quiet corridors.

Almost every morning I was there. I sat on a bench and read. Sometimes I let the book drop upon my lap, let my mind wander, listened to the sounds of Paris all around me, and enjoyed the infinite repose of these *allées* of a bygone age.

But I soon noticed I was not the only one to frequent this place when the gates opened; rounding the corner of a hedge I sometimes came face to face with a strange little old man.

He wore shoes with silver buckles, a *culotte à pont*, a coat the colour of Spanish tobacco, a piece of lace knotted around his throat for a cravat, and an unlikely grey furry hat with a large brim, which brought Noah to mind.

He was thin, very thin, angular; he grimaced, he smiled. His bright eyes darted around under constantly twitching eyelids and he always carried a superb gold-topped cane, which must have been some treasured and magnificent souvenir.

This little man astonished me at first and then interested me enormously. I spied on him through the leafy walls, I followed him from a long way off, stopping when there was a bend in the hedge, so as not to be seen.

And then, one morning, when he thought himself all alone, he began to make strange little movements: first a few little jumps, then a bow; then he executed on his skinny legs an *entrechat* that still had some life to it, then he began to twirl bravely round and round, hopping on one leg, shaking himself in a funny little way, smiling as if he were in front of an audience, making elegant little movements, arching his arms, twisting his

poor, puppet-like body, and making touching, ridiculous gestures into the air. He was dancing!

I remained rooted to the spot in astonishment,
wondering which of us was mad, me or him.

But suddenly he stopped, came forward as actors do
on stage, then retreated again, smiling graciously,
bowed, and, with a hand that trembled, blew kisses
like an actress at the two rows of pruned trees.

And then with all gravity he resumed his walk.

From that day on I did not let him out of my sight; and
every morning he began his unlikely exercises again.

I had an uncontrollable urge to speak to him.
I plucked up courage, greeted him, and said:

'A fine day, Monsieur.'

He bowed.

'Yes, Monsieur, just like in the old days.'

A week later we were firm friends, and I learned all
about him. He had been a dance tutor at the Opéra in
the time of King Louis XV. His beautiful cane was a
present from the Comte de Clermont. And when
I raised the subject of dancing, his volubility knew no
bounds.

One day he confided in me:

'I married La Castris, Monsieur. I'll introduce you if
you like, but she'll only be here later. You see, this

garden is our joy, our life. It's all that remains of the old days. We feel we should not be able to live if we didn't have it. It is both ancient and elegant, don't you think? Here I feel I can breathe an air which has not changed since my young days. My wife and I spend all our afternoons here. But I come in the morning because I get up early.'

When I had finished lunch I returned to the Luxembourg, and very soon saw my friend; he was ceremoniously offering his arm to a little old lady dressed in black, to whom he introduced me. It was La Castris, the great dancer loved by princes, loved by the king, loved by everyone in that gallant age which seems to have bequeathed to the world its atmosphere of love.

We sat down on a stone bench. It was the month of May. A flowery perfume lingered above the neat paths; the warm sun slanted through the leaves, spreading great drops of light upon us. La Castris's black dress seemed drenched with brightness.

The garden was empty. You could hear the sound of cabs in the distance.

'So tell me,' I said to the old dancer, 'what was the minuet like?'

He shuddered.

'The minuet, Monsieur, was the queen of dances, and the dance of queens, do you understand? When the kings went, the minuets went.'

And in a pompous voice, he started on a lengthy eulogy of which I could make neither head nor tail. I tried to get him to describe the steps, all the movements, the positions. He got mixed up, and became exasperated, nervous, and depressed on account of his inability to describe it to me.

Then suddenly, turning to his ancient companion, who had maintained a solemn silence:

'Elise, would you like, would you please, would you care to show Monsieur what the minuet was like?'

She looked around in every direction worriedly, then got up without a word and came to stand opposite him.

And then I saw something I shall never forget.

They moved forwards and backwards in childlike posturings, smiled at each other, poised, bowed, and hopped on one leg just like two old marionnettes made to dance by an ancient, slightly broken machine built many moons ago by a skilled artisan, in the style of the times.

And I watched, my heart troubled by strange sensations, my soul moved by an inexpressible melancholy. I seemed to be looking at a lamentable and comical apparition, at shades a century out of date. I had a desire to laugh but a need to cry.

Suddenly they stopped, they had finished the figures of the dance. For a few seconds they remained upright and facing one another, their expressions twisted in a surprising fashion. Then they threw their arms around each other, and sobbed.

Three days later I left for the provinces. I never saw them again. When I returned to Paris, two years later, the old nursery had been destroyed. What became of them without their beloved and bygone garden and its graceful, meandering, tree-lined walks?

Are they dead? Are they wandering the streets today, like exiles without hope? Are they dancing a fantastic minuet like will o'the wisps between the cypresses in a graveyard along paths between the tombs, in the moonlight?

The memory of them haunts me, obsesses me, tortures me, stays inside me like a wound. Why? I do not know.

No doubt you'll think that I am ridiculous?

Snow

Émile Zola

Towards evening a pinkish-grey cloud comes up from the horizon and gradually fills the sky. Chilly little puffs of wind make the air shiver. Then a deep silence, a soft, icy stillness, descends upon a Paris drifting into sleep. The darkened city slumbers and the snow begins to fall, slowly, slowly in the frozen serenity of space. And noiselessly the sky covers the vast, sleeping city in a pure, virgin cloth.

When Paris woke it saw that the New Year had dressed the city in white during the night. The town seemed young and virginal. No more streams in the gutters, no pavements, no blackened paving-stones: the streets were wide ribbons of white satin; the squares, the grass white with daisies. And these winter daisies had also bloomed upon the dark roofs.

Everything that jutted out, windowsills, railings, branches of trees were lightly adorned with lace.

The city seemed like a little girl, young and vulnerable, like the New Year. She had just thrown off her old clothes, her mud and her dust, and put on her beautiful gauzy skirts. She breathed sweetly, with a pure, fresh breath; she displayed her innocent finery with a childish coquetterie.

It was a surprise she was springing on her city-dwellers; she was blotting out her imperfections to please them, her virgin beauty dazzled them with her smile when they awoke. She seemed to be saying to them: 'I made myself beautiful while you were asleep. I have put on my white gown of hope, to wish you a Happy New Year.'

And now, ever since yesterday, the city has become all white and virginal again.

In the winter mornings when you push up the blinds on your window, nothing is so gloomy as the street, black with cold and damp. The air is clammy with a yellowish fog that drifts dismally against the walls.

But when snow has fallen in the night, spreading its white carpet on the ground, you give a little cry of joy and surprise. All the ugliness of winter has disappeared; each house is like a beautiful woman in white furs; roofs stand out, bright against the pale, clear sky; you are in the full flowering of the cold.

Since yesterday, Paris has been enjoying the jollity that the snow bestows upon children, young and old. We are ridiculously happy—and all because the ground is white.

In Paris there are wide cityscapes like nowhere else. Habit has made us indifferent to them. But those who wander around the city—keenly sniffing the air, looking to be moved, to be amazed—are very familiar with these places. For my part, I dearly love the stretch of the Seine between Notre Dame and the Pont de Charenton; I have never seen a horizon as strange and vast as this.

When it snows, this landscape is even larger. The Seine flows, black, sinister, between two bands of dazzling white; the quays stretch out, silent, deserted, the sky seems immense, pearl-grey, soft and bleak. And in this muddied water, rumbling through the quiet whiteness, there is a poignant melancholy, sad and bittersweet.

This morning a boat went down the river. It was full of snow and made a white blotch on the murky water—like a piece of the bank moving down with the current.

What writer would take on the job of sketching the landscapes of Paris with his pen? He would have to show how the city changes its aspect each season, black in the rain and white in the snow, clear and joyful in the first May sunshine, hot and exhausted in the heat of August.

I have just crossed the Luxembourg gardens, without recognizing either trees or borders. A far cry from the shimmering golds and greens in the red-and-yellow brightness of the setting sun. It was like being in a cemetery. The flower-beds resembled colossal marble tombs, with here and there shrubs for black crosses.

The staggered rows of chestnut trees are enormous chandeliers of spun glass. The work is exquisite; each little branch is decorated with fine crystals; delicate embroideries cover the brown bark. You dare not touch these fragile glass ornaments in case you break them.

In the long *allée*, the paths have been ripped up. Brutally, a road is to be cut through the bushes, and the workmen have already made gaping wounds in the earth. They look like common graves. The snow on the edges of these trenches makes their open mouths look sinister; they seem all black next to this whiteness as though waiting for the miserable coffins of the poor. A stranger would think the plague has just hit Paris and that they are using the Luxembourg to bury the dead.

What a desolate place! The gashed earth shows its brown entrails; the cartwheels have dug deep ruts and the dirty trodden snow lies there like a ragged cloth full of holes spread over the earth to cover up its wounds, but unable to hide the poverty and horror of it.

And the trees, the tall, spun-glass chandeliers, are the only things to retain their fine chasings; over there on the terraces the statues shiver with cold under their white cloaks, and peer over the railings at the immaculate, virgin lawns.

But there are some Parisians who are not greatly impressed by the snow. I'm talking about the sparrows, those grey, cheeky little chaps renowned for their fussing and impudence.

They don't mind the rain or dirt; they can run around in the mud without getting their feet dirty. But the poor little things utter desperate cries when they hop about in the snow searching for breadcrumbs. They are no longer appealingly chirpy and insolent; they are meek and irascible, they are starving, they can no longer recognize the good places where they can normally gorge themselves, and they fly away in fear, stiff with hunger and cold.

Ask people who live in attics. They will all tell you that, that morning, the little chaps came tapping with their beaks on the windowpane. They were asking to come in, to eat, to get warm. They are brave, trusting little souls who know what humans are like and are well aware we are not unkind. They have eaten at our feet on the streets, they can surely eat at our table when we are at home.

Those who have let them in have seen them to be soft and lively little creatures. They alight on the corner of a piece of furniture, happy to be warm, puffing their feathers, and have pecked with delight at the crumbs placed in front of them. Then, as soon as a ray of sunshine has coloured the snow rose, off they flit with a little cry of thanks.

At the Carrefour de l'Observatoire I saw a shivering but ecstatic group of children. There were three of them: two boys of about ten, wearing Neapolitan costume, and a little girl of eight, her skin browned by the sun of Naples. On a pile of snow they had placed their instruments, two harps and a violin.

The two boys were having a snowball fight and shrieking. The little girl was crouching down and shoving her hands, blue with cold, into the white ground. Her brown face looked ecstatic beneath the shred of cloth covering her head. She was gathering up her red woollen skirt in between her legs, and you could see her poor little bare legs shaking. She was frozen, and yet there was a radiant smile on her rosy lips.

No doubt these children only knew the terrible heat of the sun; this cold, the snow, smooth and biting, was a very special delight. Street-birds of passage, they came from a harsh, hot part of the world, and forgot their hunger as they played with the white blossoms of winter.

I approached the little girl.

'Aren't you afraid of the cold?' I asked.

She looked at me with a child's boldness, and her black eyes widened.

'Oh yes,' she answered in her own patois. 'My hands are stinging, it's great fun.'

'But quite soon you won't be able to hold your violin.'

That seemed to scare her and she ran to get her instrument. Then, sitting in the snow, she started to scrape the strings with all the strength of her stiff fingers. She accompanied that barbaric music with a high-pitched, jerky song which hurt my ears.

Her red skirts made a bright, warm mark on the snow. It was the sun of Naples smothered in the Paris fog.

But the city does not wear her beautiful white dress for long. Her wedding gown won't last. In the morning she decks herself in all her lace, her finest gauze and shiniest satin, and often by evening she has already soiled and torn her finery. A few days later her white dress is in tatters.

The air becomes softer, the snow bluer, thin trickles of water run along the walls, and then the thaw begins, the dreadful thaw that fills the streets with slush. The whole city exudes wet; the walls are grey and sticky, the trees seem to be rotting or dead, the gutters turn to black sewers, impossible to cross.

And Paris is muddier, gloomier, dirtier than before. She was happy to put on her best clothes, but now those clothes are rags and lie around shamefully on the cobbled streets.

La Halle

Gérard de Nerval

'What a beautiful night!' I said, seeing the stars twinkling over the vast terrain from which rose, on the left, the dome of the corn market with its cabbalistic column that was once part of the Hôtel de Soissons and that used to be called Catherine de Medici's Observatory; then, further on, the poultry market; on the right, the butter market; and beyond that, the still-unfinished meat market.—The greyish silhouette of Saint Eustache closes the scene. This admirable building, in which the exuberance of the Middle Ages and the correct designs of the Renaissance go so well together, still looks magnificent when a moon illuminates its Gothic frame, its succession of flying buttresses like the ribs of some stupendous whale, and the Romanesque arches of its doors and windows, whose ornamentation seems rather to belong to the ogival style. Such a pity that so precious a vessel should be dishonoured on the right by a sacristy door with Ionic columns and on the left by a porch in the taste of Vignola.

The little square between the markets was coming to life. There was a ceaseless to-ing and fro-ing of carts carrying seafood, salad, butter, and produce from the market-gardens. The carters arriving at their destinations took refreshments in the cafés and taverns that on this square stay open all night. In the Rue Mauconseil these places stretch as far as the oyster market, and in the Rue Montmartre from the angle of Saint Eustache to the Rue du Jour.

On the right there you'll find the leech-sellers, the other side is occupied by the Raspail pharmacies and the cider stalls—at which you can treat yourself to oysters and *tripes à la mode de Caen*. The pharmacies are useful (accidents occur); but for healthy strollers a glass of cider or perry is the thing, for refreshment.

We ordered *new* cider—only the Normans and the Bretons can enjoy the *hard*. They told us the new ciders wouldn't be in for another week, and moreover the harvest was poor.—But the perries, they said, came in yesterday. Last year there were none.

So Domfront, 'unhappy town', is a happy town this year. Their perry, white and foaming like champagne, much resembles the *blanquette* of Limoux. It is conserved in bottles, and goes to the head nicely. There is, besides, a certain cider-brandy from the same region, the price varying according to the size of the small glasses. This is what we read on a card attached to the bottle:

Gentleman:	4 sous.
Young Lady:	2 sous.
Down-and-out:	1 sou.

The brandy whose measures are denominated thus is not at all bad and will serve instead of absinthe.—It is unknown in the best restaurants.

The Market of the Innocents

Passing to the left of the fish market, which is only lively between five and six in the morning when the auctions are on, we noticed a crowd of men in smocks, round hats, and white coats striped in black. Some were lying on sacks of beans or warming themselves at fires such as soldiers make when they camp. Others were stoking up *inwardly* in one of the nearby taverns. Others, still standing by their sacks, were engaged in getting the best price for their beans . . . The talk was all of options, variations, cover, and contango—in a word, upturns and downturns, just like the stock exchange.

'Those men in smocks are richer than us,' said my companion. 'They are sham peasants. Under their carters' hats and smocks they are perfectly well dressed and tomorrow they'll leave their outfits at the vintners and drive home in their tilburies. The clever speculator puts on a smock the way a barrister puts on a robe. Those you see sleeping are the *sheep*, just carters.'

'Soissons haricots, 46–66,' a man close by said gravely. '48 at the month-end,' said another. 'Swiss whites, impossible prices.' 'Dwarf beans, 28.' 'Vetches, 13–34.' 'The flageolets are weak.' And so on.

We leave these good people to their calculations. The money won and lost in this fashion! And they banned all games of chance!

The Charnel Houses

Under the columns of the potato market, women up very early or very late were peeling their wares by lamplight. There were some pretty girls working under the surveillance of their mothers and singing old songs. Those ladies are often richer than they look, and even having made a fortune they don't give up their rough work. My companion was amusing himself in a very long conversation with a pretty blonde, speaking to her of the last ball in the markets, at which she must surely have been one of the greatest beauties... She answered him very elegantly, like a society woman, until on some inexplicable whim he turned to her mother and said, 'But your young lady is charming... *A-t-elle le sac?*' (Which in market parlance means, 'Does she have any money?') 'No, son, she doesn't,' said the mother. 'But I do.'—'Well now, madam, if you were a widow we might... We'll speak further about this.' 'Clear off, slob!' the girl yelled—in an entirely local accent quite at odds with her previous speech.

She reminded me of the blonde witch in *Faust* who, conversing tenderly with her dancing partner, suddenly spews forth a red mouse.

We turned away, pursued by mockery and curses pretty well classic Vadé in style.

'Definitely time to eat,' said my companion. 'Here's Bordier's, but it's a bit cramped. That's where the orange-dealers go and the girls from their stalls. There's another Bordier on the corner of the Rue aux Ours, which would do. Then the Restaurant des Halles, with new carvings and gilding, near the Rue de la Reynie... But the Maison d'Or would be just as good.'

'What about those over there?' I said, turning towards the line of houses, all matching, that border the part of the market given over to cabbages.

'You'd like to try there? Those are the charnel houses. That's where the poets in silk with their swords and cuffs used to come for their suppers last century on days when they had no invitations in high society. They'd eat the set meal for six sous and then their custom was to read their verses aloud to the carters, market-gardeners, and the "Strong Men". "Never did I have such success," said Robbé, "as with that audience shaped for the arts by the hands of nature."'

'After such suppers the poetical frequenters of these vaulted cellars would stretch out on the benches or the tables and the following morning they had to get themselves powdered for two sols by some poor barber in the open air and darned and mended by the local sewing girls before going off to shine at the *petits levers* of Mme de Luxembourg, Mlle Hus, or the Comtesse de Beauharnais.'

Baratte

Those days have gone.—The charnel-house cellars have been restored, gas-lighting installed. They are perfectly decent places in which to eat and drink, and neither on nor under the tables is sleeping permitted. But what a street that is for cabbages! The Rue de la Ferronnerie, running parallel, is just as full, and in Sainte-Opportune, nearby, truly there are mountains of them. Carrots and turnips are in that department too. 'Curly kale, my darlings?' a stallholder shouts at us. 'Savoys? Whites?'

Crossing the square we admire some monstrous pumpkins. We are offered sausages and black puddings—and coffee, one sou a cup—and right under the fountain of Pierre Lescot and Jean Goujon, full in the wind, a more modest clientèle than that of the charnel houses has seated itself for supper.

We close our ears to all invitations and make for Baratte's through the dense crowd of women selling fruit and flowers.—One of them shouts, 'Come along now, darlings, *flower* your ladies!' And since at that hour they only sell in bulk you'd need to have a lot of ladies to flower before you'd buy such quantities of bouquets. Another woman sings the song of her occupation:

> Golden Nobles, D'Arcy Spice
> Orleans and Bountiful
> Small and large and pink and white
>
> When I was queen in Appletown
> The men came shopping from miles around
> Come away, come away
>
> Dumelows, Encores! Encore!
> All I sold they wanted more
> Come away, come away

> I sell apples while I can
> I've a kind for every man
> Cabbages and kale can wait
>
> Till I'm grey, till I'm grey...

Deaf to the voices of these sirens, we finally reach Baratte's. An individual in a smock, 'drink taken', as they say, has just been flung out for making a row and lies wallowing among the flowers. He is settling down to sleep on a mound of red roses, doubtless supposing himself to be old Silenus and that the Bacchantes have prepared him this odorous couch. The flower-women fall on him and now his fate looks more likely to be that of Orpheus... But an officer of the law intervenes and conducts him to the station at the leather market, recognizable from afar by its bell-tower and an illuminated sign.

The big room at Baratte's is a bit boisterous, but there are separate rooms and small alcoves too. Beyond a doubt, this is the restaurant for the nobs. The usual thing is to order oysters from Ostend and a little dish of shallots chopped in vinegar with which you lightly season the said oysters. Next the onion soup, admirably well made at La Halle and into which connoisseurs sprinkle some grated Parmesan.—After that a partridge or one or another fish, needless to say obtainable at first hand, some bordeaux and a dessert of first-rate fruit, and you will agree one eats very well indeed at La Halle.—All for about seven francs each.

It seems scarcely believable that these men in smocks together with the fair sex from the suburbs in their cornets and marmots should be eating so respectably, but, as I said, these are sham peasants—millionaires you would never recognize as such. The chief agents of La Halle, the big sellers of vegetables, meat, butter, and shellfish, are people who treat themselves to the best. And the 'Strong Men' are rather like the estimable dockers of Marseilles whose capital actually supports the firms that give them work.

Paul Niquet

Supper finished, we went for coffee and a drop to chase it with at Paul Niquet's famous establishment.—Not so many millionaires there as at Baratte's, needless to say... The walls, very high with windows around the top, are entirely bare. Underfoot you have damp flagstones. The room is divided in two by an immense counter and seven or eight rag-and-bone women, regulars of the place, sit in a decorative line on a bench facing this counter. The far end is occupied by a mixed crowd, among whom arguments are not uncommon.

Since one can't be forever fetching in the Law, old Niquet, so well known under the Emperor for his cherries in brandy, installed a system of water conduits very efficacious in any violent tumult.

The pipes were opened onto the combatants at several points of the room, and if this didn't quieten them down a sort of sluice gate was raised which sealed tight the exit. Then the water-level rose and even the most furious asked for quarter. That is what happened in former times, at least.

My companion advised me that it was necessary to buy the rag-pickers a round so as to have allies in the house should there be any arguments. And besides, it is expected of anyone respectably dressed. After that you can give yourself up to the charms of the company without fear. You have won the favour of the ladies.

One of them asked for a brandy. 'You know you're not allowed that,' said the drinks waiter. 'Oh all right then, a *verjus*, Polyte, my sweetheart. What a pretty boy you are with your lovely black eyes! Oh if I was what I used to be . . .' Her shaky hand dropped the little glass of *verjus* grapes in brandy—it got picked up at once. The little glasses at Paul Niquet's are as thick as decanter stoppers: they bounce and only the drink is lost.

'Another *verjus*!' said my friend.

'And you're a pretty boy too,' the rag-picker said to him. 'You remind me of young Barras, who was such a pretty pretty boy with his pigtails and his English lace...Oh he was a one, my dear, indeed he was... And a good looker just like you!'

After the second *verjus* she said to us, 'What you don't know is I was one of the *merveilleuses* back then...I had rings on my toes...*Mirliflores* and generals fought duels over me!'

'And see how our Father in Heaven has punished you!' said a man standing nearby. 'Where's your horse and carriage now, I'd like to know?'

'Our Father in Heaven!' said the rag-picker in some exasperation. 'Our Father's the Devil.'

A thin man in a threadbare black suit, who had been sleeping on a bench, rose staggering to his feet. 'If God the Father is the Devil, then the Devil is God the Father, it comes down to the same. This good lady is guilty of a frightful fallacy,' he said, turning to us. 'How ignorant these people are! Oh education! It has been my passion for so many years. My philosophy consoles me for all that I have lost.'

'And a glass of something,' said my companion.

'Gladly, if you will permit me to draw a distinction between divine and human law...'

My head was beginning to spin in this strange gathering, but my companion was enjoying the philosopher's conversation and stood him one glass after another, to hear his reasonings and unreasonings longer.

If all these details were not accurate, and if I were not here seeking to daguerrotype reality, what funds for fiction these two types of misery and stupefaction would furnish me with! The rich do not have the courage to enter such places—halls of purgatory from which it might be possible to save a few souls... A mere writer can do no more than lay his finger on these sores without ever claiming to close them.

The priests themselves who think to save souls in China, India, or Tibet, might they not carry out their sublime and dangerous missionary work in places such as these? Why did our Lord live among heathens and publicans?

The sun is beginning to show through the upper windows of the room, the doors are lighted up. I hurry from this hell just as an arrest is being made, and with joy breathe in the scent of the flowers heaped on the pavement of the Rue aux Fers.

Around the great market are two long queues of women. The dawn lights up their pale faces. They are the retailers of the various sorts of produce. They have each been given a number and are waiting their turn to receive their goods at the day's rate.

Time to leave. I make my way to the Strasburg station, the night's vain spectres lingering in my head.

Confronting the Present

for Louis senior

Andrée Chedid

'*I'm* living in the *present!*' This expression and especially the last word was a comfort to Wallace.

It was, he thought, a good way of keeping going, staying alive. Existing. Of wiping out nostalgia, routine, habits.

He was to get his answer—unexpected, mind-blowing—that very evening in the metro.

In order to get to the Porte de Clignancourt, Wallace had to cross the whole of Paris. He found himself making that trip there in the middle of April. He'd done the same journey almost half a century before, when he'd arrived, just after the war, for a year studying at the Sorbonne.

He started counting the stations, as he used to, that he still had to pass through before he got there.

Suddenly, he didn't quite know why or how, he found himself confronted by that word *present* that he liked so much.

And in that same second the word vanished into thin air!

Wallace concentrated, plunged deep inside himself to capture the rhythm, the pulsating of this word which had shattered into little splinters.

But the *present* was suddenly wiped out. He could no longer recall it to his consciousness, even surreptitiously.

It had totally gone, slipped away. The word no longer had any substance. No weight, no texture. In spite of Wallace applying his mind and making repeated efforts to catch hold of it, it had wriggled away like an eel.

Had the present ever existed?

The same vagueness that came over him when he thought about what the cosmos looked like, when he imagined the solar and planetary system, the unfathomable mystery of life, overwhelmed Wallace and made him feel very dizzy.

It was the rush hour. It was extremely crowded in the metro. The seats were folded up to allow the stream of passengers to invade the whole compartment. For a moment Wallace doubted their existence—and then doubted his own.

But feeling against his back and his shoulders the warmth of other backs, other shoulders, and seeing that his breath mingled with other breaths, and rubbing against the surfaces of other bodies and other objects, he gradually regained his self-possession.

He squeezed his left hand very tight on one of the rails in order to experience the sensation of warmth in the metal. With his other hand he felt his salmon-coloured shirt in velvety silk that he had bought himself for this excursion, and had the same pleasurable sensation in his fingers: 'I am here, definitely here,' he told himself.

In spite of this reassurance, it was perfectly obvious that the present itself had disappeared! Time vanished, like a dove in the top hat in a magician's sleight-of-hand.

Confronted with that void, that vacuum, that nothingness, that illusion with which he sustained his days, Wallace tried to analyse, in the minutes remaining to him—the metro had just left Les Halles—the new situation.

Hardly had the word *present* occurred to him when, in one miraculous leap, it fixed itself to the past; enlarging it, reinforcing it relentlessly.

Or, quite the opposite, it was one with the future.

There was no other way out. Unless you wanted to step on to a moving walkway whose speed or destination was impossible to measure, you had to opt for one or the other.

It was a matter of urgency—the metro was arriving at Gare du Nord—to think of the 'present' strictly as an empty shell, a bubble. Or no, not even an empty shell or a bubble: those did at least have some shape to them!

First and foremost, entertain the notion that the present was nothing. Nothing at all. Then, between the past and the future, stake out one's position.

It would indeed have been worrying to remain without any points of reference.

The past—History excepted—his own past did not inspire him.

Although Wallace had achieved a good few goals in the course of his long life, this past seemed to him very tiny, anecdotal, absurdly subjective.

Moreover, the recounting by others of memories they had in common was so muddied with errors and cluttered up with personal feelings that he did not recognize himself in these either murky or flatteringly ethereal accounts of the past.

The 'once' looked like a trap, a lure. Until now he had chosen to stride over it, forge ahead. 'I live in the present!' he repeated. But since the present didn't exist, or no longer existed, should he then neglect the past and go with the future?

His own, and it was pointless to deny it, was shrinking, getting smaller as he looked.

Wallace had reached that point in his reflections when the metro stopped at the terminus.

He left the train, climbed the steps, up and up. As he did so, he said to himself that he must have missed the escalator; but was there one at the Porte de Clignancourt?

At the exit, a young man with a lot of hair and a leather jacket held the door open for him. He hurried through, thanked him; at the same time sorry to leave behind that very special smell of the Paris metro. A sharp-sweet odour which he sometimes caught a whiff of back home in his house in the woods.

Outside he bought a newspaper at the kiosk and waited for Pauline. He always arrived early.

For a few seconds he havered between the desire to see her again and the wish to plunge back into the metro so as not to look at the face of his friend as she was now. It was a cruel fact that her face could now only be a mask over what she had looked like at twenty.

But since he had come from such a long way away for this meeting, he decided to stay and face up to it.

From the other side of the road, Pauline was already calling him.

'Hey Wallace, Willy, It's me.'

She took the initiative, fearing he would not recognize her under the ruinous deceits of age. He took comfort from the fact that she had recognized him so promptly.

'Pauline, Linou!'

He crossed the pavement and went to meet her.

'As handsome as ever,' she said, kissing him lightly on the cheek.

He took both of her hands, pressed them to his lips, planted a kiss, as he always used to do, on each wrist. The bracelet he had given her was on her arm.

'I always wear it.'

'The past,' he sighed.

'It's still the present.'

He was tempted to tell her about his recent experience, but she was taking so much pleasure in this reunion he didn't want to spoil anything by talking.

He leaned forward, carefully removed her tortoiseshell glasses, and looked into her eyes.

'Blue as ever,' he remarked, with satisfaction.

She was smiling. He was too.

Something indefinable was happening between them. Something which threw a bridge up over the years. A tremor, a rush of blood they thought had been laid to rest.

It made them attractive to one another despite their wrinkles, poignant in spite of their slightly increased girth.

Holding hands, they walked towards their old café.

The lighting had changed; the owners too. The tables, with their marble tray-tops and bent legs, were the same.

They sat down face to face.

'Just like in the past,' he murmured.

'Just like in the *present*,' she countered.

Again he wanted to tell her what had just happened to him. To unveil the reality, or the irreality, of that word, of that state, which she seemed to be abusing in her turn.

He held back once more. Asked:

'How has it been, all these years?'

'Difficult. I'll tell you all about it. What about you?'

'It's a long time ago . . .'

'You haven't changed,' she said. 'You only ever loved the present. Remember...'

'He thought he detected a note of reproach in her voice; what event was she seeking to remind him of?

'Shall we have some lunch?' he said abruptly, avoiding the question.

'Of course. I'm free. What about you?'

'Me too.'

'How long are you staying?'

'As long as I like.'

They shared their bread, their wine, their laughter.

At the end of the meal, a silence filled with happiness pervaded all. The customers and their surroundings were dissolving into the shadows.

The marble table-top, cleared, was bare. Elbows on the table they gazed fixedly and for a long time into each other's eyes.

So long, so attentively, that the seasons got mixed up, melted into one another.

So long, so deep, that the present suddenly became eternity.

The Cab

Théodore de Banville

Here is a Paris tale our forefathers would have loved to tell to raise a laugh, had there been cabs in the days of King Louis XI. There is a moral in it, and it is this: that there may be a thousand varied and infinitely different ways of getting a woman to love you—with sighs, jokes, little attentions, exquisite dishes, or by a generous supply of rare pearls—but the easiest way to lose one is to show you are a coward, albeit only for a minute.

Everyone knows of Janoty, the writer of musicals. Although he is as poor as Job and his work has only so far been put on at the Folies-Marigny, this worthy but pasty-looking man, cursed with one of those faces that Heinrich Heine called *superfluous*, was, only a month ago, loved and respected and in possession of something much rarer than words that rhyme with *triomphe*: a faithful wife! Now he is no different from Sganarelle, except that imagination plays no part in his case. Viewed from any angle, he is a horned beast; when he walks along the street it's as though a whole forest is on the move; such thick branches grow on his forehead you might hear the nightingales sing amongst them, and he wouldn't be able to walk under triumphal arches without lowering his head. Any children he has will be, not just 'somebody's sons', as Figaro demands, but the sons of everyone; for Mme Janoty, pretty, charming little Colette, warms her irons in a fire which never dies down and throws her cap at windmills that never cease to turn!

In pious memory of her grandmother Eve, she buries her lovely little snowy-white teeth into mounds of green apples, and she is in regular conversation with the Serpent. In the Bois de Boulogne, if you see the blind on a carriage lowered, and a pert little light-brown head disappearing behind it, that vanished profile is hers. If in a passageway you should happen to meet a woman with a shapely body, heavily veiled and muffled, ringing a bachelor's doorbell, that's Colette again. It is she going up the stairs of the Café Anglais and coming down at the Maison d'Or. In short, she is in a thousand places but never at home. You will see her behind the screens in a box at the theatre, at the village ball, on the dance-floor, and everywhere that Love, the clever huntsman, makes ready his lime and his lures. As for Janoty, he bites his nails from morning till night, with such determination he soon won't have any left. Such is his tragic destiny, and as you will see, he has asked for it!

Colette was an adorable little woman, doing her best to believe in her husband's genius, keeping her house clean and tidy without the help of a maid, scraping and saving, making exquisite dishes out of nothing at all, always amiable, pleasant, cheerful, playing Janoty's works on the piano whenever he wished, a hundred times in a row; warming up the boiled beef next day with sauces fit for a king, perfect, divine, entirely out of her own head; and in the heat of the day she would sometimes go up to the market at Batignolles, where from time to time you can buy prawns for a song! Janoty was perfectly happy, loved, spoiled, looked after and fed most royally. Colette, with her large sensual eyes, her pomegranate lips, and the Arab blood in her veins on her mother's side, would sometimes breathe sighs fit to move stones, and dreamed about a poet black as a mole, who followed her around in the streets and threw her the glances of a drowning man; but she clung to her sense of duty.

Today she has trampled those feelings under her little high-heeled shoes, and danced upon them! If Janoty needed a pseudonym, he could, without laying himself open to any complaint, call himself Maître Cornelius, and there are several dozen Parisians whom he might quite justifiably address as 'Monsieur and Cher Confrère'. How did things come to this pass, and so irrevocably, in less than five minutes? That's what I am about to divulge.

La Grande Tata, star of the Folies-Marigny, who lacks neither Madame Judic's modesty, nor Jeanne Granier's indecent way with words, nor Madame Théo's candyfloss hair, and will become as famous as anyone if it pleases Fairy Carabosse who presides over absurdities; this slim, elegant, blonde, frivolous Tata had a sudden passion for the song, 'Mon frère pompe pompe pompe, car il est pompier', and came to ask Janoty if he would write a number for her new show that would be (and yet would not quite be) 'Mon frère pompe pompe pompe'. Our maestro has exactly the kind of talent required for this sort of transposition; so he could produce any amount of what La Patti wanted at any time. It was Colette who opened the door to her; she was peeling vegetables with her usual thoroughness and had a dishcloth in her hand. 'Tell him I am here,' said Tata, with a flick of her train; and the obedient

Colette did so. While Tata was in the middle of dazzling Janoty, of whirling and twirling before his dazed eyes and making him see any number of stars, it started to rain like last month, when it ruined many a hat and brought into blossom many a rose. 'Good gracious, it's pouring down,' said La Grande Tata. 'Have your maid send for a cab!'

Janoty then had a golden opportunity to prove himself a worthy or even a decent man, and to say: 'I have no maid; that's my wife.' But he was cowardly and said: 'With pleasure!' So, twiddling his thumbs, he went into the dining-room, which served as a reception room, where Colette was peeling her vegetables for all she was worth, cleaning and scraping like the good little housewife she was. 'You know,' he murmured, 'Mlle Tata is wearing a satin dress, and satin shoes, and it's raining cats and dogs, would you be so good as to ...'

'... get her a cab?' said Colette, throwing a sharp, blazing look at her husband which ought to have made him crawl under a stone. 'Get a cab? But of course! Straight away!'

She went out, wetting her only pair of boots right in the middle of the gutter, and even accepted the twenty sous that La Grande Tata slipped her for her trouble. And it was from then on that Janoty's curiosity, if he had any, must surely have been satisfied, for every day, without so much as stirring from his house, he could witness a pantomime in 150 tableaux, with changes of scenery before his very eyes, odder than the Funambules. He learned what it was like to have cold soup, warmed-up wine, dripping candles instead of lamps, and, when he sat down at the table, a slice of cold meat for his supper brought to the table in a piece of wrapping-paper. Colette, who once used to rise at dawn, had to be dragged out of bed at eleven, sighing: 'Oh, is it light?' The once gleaming household, where you would have had trouble discovering a speck of dust, now looked like an Italian town taken by the Vandals. There were spiders' webs on the plates and saucepans on the clock; no buttons on suits or shirts; only holes, on the other hand, in socks! But that was nothing. Janoty belonged to the school of the Tune, which is to say that he expressed human emotions by copying out 'J'ai du bon tabac', the 'Menuet d'Exaudet', and 'Marie trempe ton pain dans la sauce!' Before his wrongdoing, Colette had flattered this little passion of his. But now she let rip and threw aside all pretence: she played nothing but Wagner!

Her nervous fingers evoked thunderous hurricanes; the piano resounded with Tannhausers, Valkyries, Rheingolds, Twilights of the Gods. Swan-maidens emerged from it, Venuses confined in their castles and monster-slaying knights in golden armour studded with blue lizards. In the middle of all this din Janoty thought he could see the ironic Berlioz with his parrot's nose, perched on a bookshelf flinging curses punctuated by cymbals at him. He could also see skin-and-bones Wagner in sulphur-yellow damask trousers and pink dressing-gown, spreading bat-like wings, as if to carry him away to some sabbath on the Brocken. But when he clutched his brow in despair and said: 'This music is giving me a fearful headache,' Colette replied sweetly: 'I went out to get the cab!' And that phrase became the refrain in all their exchanges. 'Colette, the soup is cold'—'I went out to get the cab'—'There are no buttons on my shirt'—'I went out to get the cab'—'You don't love me any more, you don't kiss me any more'—'No, my dear, but I did go out to get the cab.'

Need I say that Colette had begun by more than gratifying the desires of the young poet, dark as a mole; but she had very rapidly provided him with as many successors as there are lapis-lazuli eyes on the tail of a peacock! Her ultimate pleasure lay in proceeding to tear away the scales from Janoty's eyes. She went bathing at an hour when the baths were shut, she went to look after aunts who had been dead for thirty years, and invited herself to plays in all the theatres where nothing was being put on. Dresses fifty francs a metre grew naturally upon her back, like wings on angels; diamonds and precious stones lighted up spontaneously on her ears and bosom, and drawers filled all by themselves with cambric blouses trimmed with lace and boxes of gloves with thirty buttons. However, Colette decided that she had not yet rubbed it in enough, and so she piled on yet more.

She appeared morning, noon, and night, in sunshine and in gaslight, out on the boulevards, with lovers—young, old, big, small, ugly, handsome, and others with nothing special to recommend them; she sat at tables in the cafés, she went for rides in open carriages; she dined in restaurants, and, coming back home, she left her love-letters open and lying around, to such an extent that finally her husband got to noticing that something was wrong. Once stung by the horsefly of jealousy, he read her letters, followed the carriages, found out about it all from people in his neighbourhood and elsewhere, and the day came when he knew the whole tale by heart. He accumulated proof, wrote notes, got together files; when he had done all that, he made Colette sit down, just like Augustus with Cinna, and made a formal indictment, starting with the words: 'Madame, you have deceived me!' Once under way he went through it all, the numbers of the rooms, the names of the lovers and of the men who hired the carriages, and everything else besides! During this oration, Colette was rosy as a peach, gay as a thrush, cheerful as an April morning, and, as Janoty detailed her misdemeanours, his noble words punctuated by sobs, and blamed her for having, with the utmost violence, torn holes in her marriage contract, she replied with irrepressible delight: 'That's true, my dear, you are quite right, but . . . I did go out and get that cab!'

The Little Restaurant at Ternes

A Christmas tale for grown-ups

Georges Simenon

The hands on the clock with the black casing, which customers had always known to hang in that place above the pigeonholes where the serviettes were kept, pointed to four minutes to nine. The advertising calendar behind the till, just above the head of Mme Bouchet, the cashier, showed 24 December.

Outside it was drizzling. In the café it was warm. In the middle of the floor stood a big stove like the ones you used to see in stations, its black pipe rising high before disappearing into the wall.

Mme Bouchet, her lips moving, was counting out the banknotes. The *patron* watched her composedly, the grey cloth bag into which he put the contents of his cash till each evening already in his hand.

Albert the waiter looked at the time, went over to them, winked, pointed to a bottle that stood apart from the others on the counter. The patron looked at the clock too, shrugged his shoulders, and nodded assent.

'Even if they are the last, that's no reason why we shouldn't give them some, just as we do the others,' Albert muttered, taking the tray.

He often talked to himself when he was serving customers.

The *patron*'s car was waiting outside by the kerb. He lived a long way away in Joinville, where he had had a house built. His wife had been a cashier. He had been a waiter. As a result he had sore feet, like all waiters and *mâitres d'hôtel*, and he wore special shoes. The back of his car was full of parcels, prettily tied with ribbons, that he would take back for the New Year.

The cashier would catch the bus for the Rue Caulaincourt, where she would celebrate Christmas at her daughter's; she was married to someone who worked at the Hôtel de Ville.

Albert had two children, and their toys had been hidden for several days on top of the big wardrobe.

He began with the man; putting a small glass on the table, he filled it with Armagnac.

'Compliments of the season from the *patron*,' he said.

Passing several empty tables, he reached the corner where Big Jeanne had just lit her cigarette and, carefully positioning himself between her and the till, he muttered:

'Drink up quickly, so I can give you another one! It's on the house.'

He finally reached the end of the line of tables. A girl was taking a lipstick out of her handbag and was looking at herself in a small mirror.

'Compliments of the season from the house...'

She looked at him in surprise.

'This is what we do here at Christmas.'

'Thank you.'

He would have been happy to pour two glasses for her as well, but he didn't know her well enough and she was too near the cash-desk.

Right! Another glance at the *patron* to check if it were time to go and pull down the shutters. It was already very good of him to have waited this long for the customers. In most Paris restaurants, at that time, they would be frantically preparing the tables for the

Christmas dinners. But this was a little establishment for locals, with a fixed-price menu, a quiet restaurant, not far from Place des Ternes, in the least frequented part of Faubourg Saint-Honoré.

There had not been many diners that night. More or less everyone had family or friends. Only those three were left, two women and a man, and the waiter hadn't the heart to tell them to go. For them to be dawdling like that after their plates were cleared away, there must have been nobody expecting them back.

He closed the shutter on the left, then the shutter on the right, and came in again, hesitating to pull down the one on the door which would mean the last customers lowering their heads to get out. Yet it was nine o'clock. The till was shut. Mme Bouchet was putting on her black hat and her coat and the little sable fur round her neck, and looking around for her gloves. The *patron* was shuffling around, his feet turned out. Jeanne was still smoking her cigarette and the girl had clumsily made her lips look thicker with the lipstick.

They were about to close. It was time. Closing time. The *patron* was on the verge of uttering, as nicely as possible, his traditional:

'Ladies and gentlemen...'

But before he could say one word, there was a sharp report and the only male customer, his eyes open wide, and, one would have said, full of absolute astonishment, swayed to and fro before slumping sideways on to the bench.

Casually, without any word or warning, precisely at closing-time, he had just fired a bullet into his head.

'You'd better hang on for a few minutes,' said the *patron* to the two women. There's a local policeman on the street corner. Albert's gone to fetch him.'

Jeanne had risen to go and look at the dead man and, standing by the stove, she lit another cigarette. The girl, in her corner, was chewing her handkerchief and, in spite of the heat, was trembling all over.

The policeman arrived, his cape glistening with raindrops. He smelled of the barracks.

'Do you know him?'

'He's been coming here to eat every day for years. He's Russian.'

'Are you sure he's dead? If so we'd better wait for the inspector. I've told someone to let him know.'

They hadn't long to wait. The police station was close by in Rue de l'Étoile. The inspector was wearing an overcoat, which was either badly cut or had shrunk in the rain, and a scruffy hat, and appeared to be in a bad mood.

'The first of the night,' he grumbled, leaning over him. 'He's early. Usually it comes over them at around midnight when the party's in full swing.'

He straightened up again, holding a wallet, opened it, took out a thick green identity card.

'Alexis Borine, fifty-six years old, born in Vilna...'

He muttered under his breath, like a priest saying mass, or like Albert when he was talking to himself.

'...Hotel de Bordeaux, rue Brey...engineer...Was he an engineer?' he asked the *patron*.

'He may have been, a long time ago, but ever since he's been coming here he's appeared in films. I've recognized him several times in the cinema.'

'Any witnesses?' asked the inspector, turning round.

'Me, my cashier, the waiter, and these two ladies. If you'd like to take their names first...'

The policeman found himself face to face with Big Jeanne, who was indeed big, bigger than him by half a head.

'You, is it? Your papers...'

She held out her card. He copied down:

'Jeanne Chartrain, twenty-eight years old, out of work...Well now! Out of work, are we?'

'That's what they put at the town-hall.'

'Have you got your other card?'

She nodded.

'In order?'

'Charming man,' she smiled.

'And you?'

He turned to the girl with the badly applied make-up, who stammered:

'I haven't got my identity card on me. I'm called Martine Cornu. I'm nineteen and I was born in Yport...'

A quiver ran through Jeanne, the beanpole, who looked at her now with rather more interest. Yport was very near her home, not five kilometres away. And there were a lot of Cornus in the area. It was a Cornu who had the biggest café in Yport, on the beach.

'Address?' grumbled Inspector Lognon, who round there was known as 'the surly inspector'.

'I live in furnished accommodation in Rue Brey, number 17.'

'I expect you'll be summoned to the police station at some point. You can go.'

He was waiting for the municipal ambulance. The cashier asked:

'May I go too?'

'If you like.'

Then, as she was leaving, he called Jeanne back who was making for the door.

'You never had anything to do with this man?'

'I went upstairs with him a while ago, must have been six months back . . . At least six months, because it was at the beginning of the summer . . . He was the type who goes with a woman so he can talk to her rather than anything else, asks lots of questions, thinks you must be unhappy . . . Since then he never came over to say hello, but he always gave me a little wave when he came in.'

The young girl left. Jeanne went out hard on her heels. She was wearing a shabby fur coat that was much too short for her. She always dressed in clothes that were much too short, everyone told her so, but she carried on doing it without quite knowing why, and it made her appear even taller.

Her 'home' was fifty metres away to the right, in the total dark of Square du Roule, where there was nothing but artists' studios and little one-storey houses. She had a small flat on the first floor, with a private staircase, and a door on to the street, of which she had the key.

She had promised herself that she would go home early that evening. She never stayed out on Christmas Eve. She had hardly any make-up on, wore the simplest clothes. So much so that she had been shocked just now to see the girl slapping on her lipstick.

She went a little way in the direction of her side-street, perched on high heels, hearing their click-clack on the cobbles. Then she decided she must be feeling depressed because of the Russian. She had an urge to walk in a brightly lit place, to hear noise, and she made her way to Place des Ternes, at the beginning of the broad, well-lit avenue leading to Étoile. The cinemas, the theatres, the restaurants were all bright with lights. Posters in the café windows advertised the price and the menu of Christmas dinners, and on all the doors was the word *complet*.

The pavements were almost unrecognizeable, there were so few people on them.

The girl was walking ten metres ahead of her, as if she didn't know where to go, and she stopped from time to time in front of a shop-window or at the end of a street, unable to make up her mind whether to cross or not, looking for a long time at the photographs displayed in the warm foyer of a cinema.

'She looks as if she's the one walking the streets!'

When he saw the Russian, Lognon had grunted:

'The first of the night . . . He's early!'

Perhaps it was so as not to do the deed in the street, where it was still more gloomy, or in the solitude of his hotel room. In the restaurant there was a peaceful, almost family atmosphere. You were surrounded by familiar faces. It was warm. And indeed, the *patron* had just offered everyone drinks, with his compliments.

She shrugged. She had nothing to do. She too stopped in front of the displays, the photographs; the lighted neon signs coloured her now red, now green or purple, and she realized that the girl was still walking ahead of her.

For all she knew, she might have known her when she was a child. There were ten years between them. When she worked at the Fisheries, in Fécamp—she was already rather tall, but also thin—she often went dancing at Yport with the boys on a Sunday. Sometimes she danced at the Cornu's place, where there were always kids crawling over the floor.

'Mind the slugs,' she would say to her young men.

She called the kids 'slugs'. Her brothers and sisters were slugs too. She had six or seven then, but very likely there weren't as many as that now.

It was strange to think that the girl was in all probability a slug from Cornu's place!

Over the shops on the avenue there were flats, and almost all had their lights on; she looked up at them, refreshing her upturned face in the light drizzle, seeing the occasional shadow pass behind the curtains. What are they doing, she wondered.

They must have been reading the paper and waiting for midnight, or else dressing their Christmas trees. Some housewives would be entertaining guests and worrying about cooking the dinner.

Thousands of children would be sleeping, or pretending they were. And almost all the people crowding into the cinemas and theatres would have their tables in the restaurant booked for Christmas Eve or their seats in the church reserved for midnight mass.

For you had to book your seat in the church as well. Otherwise, might she have gone herself?

The people she met were already in jolly groups, or pairs, more closely entwined, you would have said, than on other days.

And the ones walking on their own were in more of a hurry than on other days. You felt they were going somewhere, that someone was expecting them.

Was that the reason the Russian had put a bullet through his head? And why the surly inspector asserted there would be more to come?

It was certainly the day for it! The girl, ahead of her, had stopped at the end of Rue Brey. The third house along was a hotel, and there were others, discreet establishments where you could go for a short while. It was indeed there that Jeanne had had her first encounter with a man. In the neighbouring hotel, probably right at the top—for only the worst rooms were let by the month or by the week—the Russian had lived until today.

What was the Cornu girl looking at? Big Emily? She had no shame, nor religion, that girl. There she was, despite it being Christmas, and she didn't even bother to walk up and down and make any pretence of attracting the clients. She stood by the entrance, with the words 'Furnished Rooms' displayed just above her purple hat. It's true she was old, at least forty, and had got very fat, and her feet, as sore as the *patron*'s, had had enough of carrying all that weight.

'Salut, Jeanne!' she shouted from across the road.

Big Jeanne didn't answer. Why was she following the girl? No reason. Probably because she had nothing to do and was afraid to go home, that was all.

The Cornu girl didn't know where she was going either. She had turned down Rue Brey for no particular reason, and was walking along quietly, taking short steps, dressed in a tight blue suit far too light for the season.

She was pretty. Rather plump, with a funny little bottom that wiggled as she walked. Looking at her full on in the restaurant you could see her breasts bulging in her blouse.

'If someone accosts you, my girl, you'll have asked for it!'

Especially this evening. Because respectable people, the ones with family, friends, or even just relatives, don't go out walking the streets.

The little fool didn't know that. Perhaps she wasn't even aware of what big Emily was doing at the hotel door. As she passed in front of the bars she sometimes stood on tiptoe to peer inside.

Yes, she was going in! Albert had been wrong to give her drink. Jeanne used to be like that too. If she was so unfortunate as to have one glass, she would need another. And when she had drunk three she didn't know what she was doing any more. But my goodness, it wasn't like that now! She could put away a good few now before she'd had her fill!

The bar was called Chez Fred. There was a long mahogany counter, with those barstools on which women can't perch without showing a lot of leg. It was more or less empty. Just a character at the back, a musician or a performer, already in tails, who would have to go and work in a little while in a cabaret in the area. He was eating a sandwich and drinking a glass of beer.

Martine Cornu hoisted herself on to a stool near the entrance, next to the wall, and Jeanne went to sit a little way away.

'Armagnac,' she ordered, since that was what she'd had before.

The girl was looking at all the bottles which, with the lighting underneath them, formed a subtle rainbow of different colours.

'A benedictine...'

The man behind the bar turned the knob on the wireless and a sentimental tune pervaded the café.

Why not ask her if she was one of the Yport Cornus? There were Cornus at Fécamp as well, cousins, but they were butchers in Rue du Havre.

The musician—or dancer—at the back, had already spotted Martine and was sending languorous looks in her direction.

'Have you got any cigarettes?'

She wasn't used to smoking, that much was evident from her way of opening the packet and blinking away the smoke when she exhaled.

It was ten o'clock. Another two hours till midnight. Everyone would hug and kiss one another. The verses of 'Christians Rejoice' would issue forth from the wireless in every home and everyone would sing along.

It was rather stupid, when all was said and done. Jeanne, so ready to talk to absolutely anybody, felt incapable of approaching this girl from her home area, whom she had probably known as a child.

Yet it would have been very nice. She would have said to her:

'If you're on your own as well and have had a drink or two, do you think it would be good to spend Christmas Eve together?'

She knew how to behave. She wouldn't discuss men with her, nor her job. They must have plenty of common acquaintances in Fécamp and Yport they could talk about. And why not invite her back to her flat?

Her lodgings were well-kept. She had slummed it long enough in furnished rooms to know the value of a little place on her own. She wouldn't be ashamed to show the girl her home, for she never took a man back there. Others did. But for Jeanne it was a matter of principle. And not many apartments were as clean as hers. There were even soft slippers by the door which she put on when it was rainy so as not to dirty the floor, which shone like an ice rink.

They'd buy a bottle or two, something good and not too strong. The delicatessens were still open, selling patés, lobster in a scallop shell, lovely, delicious things that you didn't get to eat every day.

She observed her covertly. Perhaps in the end she would have spoken to her if the door had not opened to admit two men, the kind Jeanne didn't like, the kind who look all around them when they arrive as if they owned the place.

'Salut, Fred,' said the smaller of the two, who was also the fatter.

They had already sized up the bar. An indifferent glance at the musician at the back, a brief glance at Jeanne who, when she was sitting down, looked less of a beanpole than she did when standing—which was also why she more often than not worked in cafés.

Of course they knew what she was. But they didn't stop staring at Martine, and sat down next to her.

'Mind if we join you?'

She huddled a little closer to the wall, still clumsily holding her cigarette.

'What you having, Willy?'

'The usual.'

'The usual, Fred.'

They were the kind of men who often speak with a foreign accent, about racing, or else discuss cars; the kind of men who, at a given moment, will wink at someone and take him to the back of the café to whisper in his ear. And who, wherever they are, need to phone someone.

The barman was preparing a complicated concoction for them. They watched him closely.

'The Baron been in?'

'He asked if one of you would ring him. He's at Francis's.'

The fatter of the two went into the phone-booth. The other one moved nearer to Martine.

'Not good for the stomach,' he remarked, clicking open his gold cigarette-lighter.

She looked at him in astonishment, and Jeanne wanted to call out:

'Don't say anything, girl!'

For once she'd said anything it would be hard for her to shake him off.

'What's bad for the stomach?'

She fell for it, little fool.

She even attempted to smile, no doubt because she had been taught to smile when she spoke to people, or perhaps because she thought if she did she would look like someone on the cover of a magazine.

'What you are drinking!'

'It's benedictine.'

She was definitely from the Fécamp area! She thought she was quite something when she said 'benedictine'.

'Thought so. Nothing like it for making you ill! Fred!'

'Yes, Monsieur Willy.'

'Another one for the young lady. Dry.'

'Right you are.'

'But...' she started to object.

'I'm only being friendly, don't worry. Is it or isn't it Christmas Eve?'

The fat one, coming out of the booth and straightening his tie in the mirror, had already twigged what was going on.

'Do you live round here?'

'Not far.'

'Barman!' called Big Jeanne. 'The same for me.'

'Armagnac?'

'No. What you just gave them.'

'A side-car?'

'If that's what it is.'

She was very angry, without any reason.

'You, my girl, you haven't got long before you'll be drunk as a skunk... Not very clever, are you!... If you were thirsty, couldn't you have picked a more suitable café? Or had a drink at home?'

It was true she hadn't been home either. And she was used to living on her own. Does anyone want to go home on Christmas Eve when they know there's nobody to go home to and that in bed they'll hear music and merrymaking from all the neighbours?

In a little while the cinemas and theatres would disgorge an impatient crowd who would rush to the thousands of tables booked in places even quite far off and in the most modern restaurants. Celebration dinners at any price!

Only no one could book a table for one. Wouldn't that be insulting to others in a group having a good time, if you went and sat in a corner and watched them? What would it look like? That you were blaming them! You would see them lean over and whisper to one another and wonder if they should invite you to join them, out of pity.

But you can't walk the streets either, or the police will follow you and look at you suspiciously, wondering if you are going to take advantage of some dark corner to do what the Russian did; or if, in a little while, despite the cold, someone might have to throw himself into the Seine and fish you out.

'What do you think of it?'

'It's not very strong.'

Being a daughter of a bar-owner she should have known better. But all women say that. You'd think they expect to be swallowing fire. So, as it's not as strong as they were anticipating, they stop being wary.

'Work in a shop?'

'No.'

'Typist?'

'Yes.'

'Been in Paris long?'

He had teeth like a film star and two little commas for a moustache.

'Do you like dancing?'

'Sometimes.'

How stupid! What pleasure was there in exchanging such mindless remarks with people like that. Did the girl really take them to be men of the world? The gold cigarette case she was proffered, not to mention the Egyptian cigarettes, must have impressed her, likewise the ring with the huge diamond on the hand of the man next to her.

'Another one here, Fred.'

'Not for me thanks. Anyway it's time I was...'

'Time you were...?'

'I'm sorry?'

'It's time you were...doing what? Surely you're not going to go to bed at ten-thirty on Christmas Eve?'

It's funny, but when you see that scene taking place without being a participant, you could weep at the stupidity of it. But when you have a part in it...

'Little feather-brain!' grumbled Jeanne, who was chain-smoking and continued to stare fixedly at the three of them.

Martine, of course, did not dare admit she was going to go to bed.

'Got a date?'

'Don't be so quizzy.'

'Boyfriend?'

'None of your business.'

'Just that I should love to keep him waiting!'

'Why?'

Jeanne knew exactly what each would say next. She knew it all by heart. She had intercepted the look given to the barman which meant:

'Step up the dose!'

But it would have been useless to serve even the stiffest cocktail to the former slug from Yport; in the state she was in she would have found it to her liking. So wasn't there enough lipstick on her lips? She felt the need to put some more on, to open her bag, to show that it was a Houbigant lipstick; and also because of the pout, because when they push out their lips towards that indecent little instrument, women believe they are irresistible.

'You're such a little fool! If you looked in the mirror you'd see that of the two of us you're the one who looks like a tart.'

Well, not quite, because it's not by being more or less plastered in make-up that you can tell. The proof is that the two men, when they came in, had only needed the briefest of glances to reach a conclusion about Big Jeanne.

'Do you know the *Monico*?'

'No, what's that?'

'Hey, Albert, she doesn't know the *Monico*!'

'You're joking!'

'And you like dancing! But darling...'

Jeanne was expecting that word, but not quite so soon. The man had been a quick worker. His leg was already pressing against one of the girl's legs and she couldn't move it away, squashed as she was against the wall.

'It's one of the most swinging nightclubs in Paris. People can't stay away. Bob Alisson jazz. You don't know Bob Alisson either?

'I don't go out very much.'

The two men exchanged winks. Also ominous. Quite soon the little fat one would remember that he had an urgent meeting with somebody and leave the field clear for his friend.

'None of that, boys,' Jeanne decided.

She too had just drunk three glasses, one after the other, not counting the two armagnacs from the *patron* in the restaurant. She wasn't drunk, she wasn't ever completely drunk, but she was beginning to think certain things important.

For instance, that this silly young girl was from her part of the country and that she was a 'slug'. Then she thought of Big Emily stuck there in the doorway of the hotel. And it was in that same hotel, though not on Christmas night, that she had gone with a man for the first time.

'Would you give me a light?'

She had slid off her stool and gone over to the smaller of the two men with her fag in her mouth.

He also knew what that meant and wasn't very pleased, he looked her up and down with a critical eye. Standing up, he must have been a good head shorter than her and she walked like a man.

'Aren't you buying me a drink?'

'If you insist ... Fred!'

'Okay.'

The silly little goose, meanwhile, was looking at her with something like indignation, as if she were being robbed.

'Come on boys, don't look so glum!'

And Jeanne, her hand on the nearer man's shoulder, began to bellow out the song playing softly on the radio.

'Little tart!' she kept saying to herself every ten minutes. 'Not one clue ...'

The strangest thing was that the little tart carried on looking at her with the utmost disdain.

Meanwhile Willy's arm had completely disappeared around Martine's waist, and the hand with the diamond signet-ring was crushed up against her breasts.

She was sprawling—yes, sprawling—across one of the crimson seats of the *Monico*, and nobody had to put her glass back in her hand now, for she was the one asking for it to be filled more often than she should have, and drinking the sparkling champagne straight off.

After each glass she burst out laughing, a measured laugh, then pressed closer to her companion.

Not yet midnight! Most tables were free. Sometimes the couple were alone on the floor and Willy was nuzzling the fine hair of the girl, his lips brushing the soft skin on the back of her neck...

'You're mad at me, aren't you!' said Jeanne, to her companion.

'Why?'

'Because you've not won the jackpot. Do you think I'm too tall?'

'A bit.'

'You can't tell when I'm lying down.'

It was a sentence she had uttered thousands of times. It was almost a slogan, as stupid as the lovey-dovey things the other two were saying to each other, but at least she wasn't saying it for her own amusement.

'Do you like Christmas parties?'

'Not specially.'

'Do you think some people really enjoy them?'

'I suppose so . . .'

'Just now in the restaurant where I was eating, a guy in the corner shot himself, very nicely, as if he was sorry to disturb us and mess up the floor.'

'Can't you tell me anything more amusing?'

'Right, order another bottle. I'm thirsty.'

It was all she could do now. Get the slug filthy drunk, since she had made up her mind not to grasp what was happening. Let her get very ill, let her be sick, there was nothing for it except to get her to bed.

'Your health, love! And good health to all the Cornus of Yport and that region.'

'Are you from round there?'

'From Fécamp. At one time I used to go dancing at Yport every Sunday.'

'That'll do!' interrupted Willy. 'We're not here for family history . . .'

Not long before, in the bar in the Rue Brey, you might have thought that one more glass would have done for the girl. But now the opposite was the case. Perhaps having a breath of fresh air had set her on her feet again. Perhaps it was the champagne. The more she drank the livelier she became. She was no longer the young girl in the little restaurant, not at all.

Willy was by now stuffing lighted cigarettes into her mouth and she was drinking from his glass. It was disgusting. And that hand moving constantly over her blouse and skirt!

In another few minutes they would all embrace, that dirty swine would press his lips to the girl's lips and she would be stupid enough to swoon into his arms.

'That's what we're like at that age! Christmas ought to be banned . . . !'

And all the other festivals as well . . . ! It was Jeanne whose eyes had started to glaze over.

'Supposing we tried another bar?'

Perhaps the fresh air this time would have the opposite effect and Martine would finally cave in. But if that happened, this pathetic playboy certainly must not try to take her home and go in with her!

'It's so nice here . . .'

And Martine, viewing her suspiciously, was talking about her in a low voice to her companion. No doubt she was saying:

'What business is it of hers? Who is she? She looks like a . . .'

The jazz stopped abruptly. A few seconds' silence. People rose to their feet.

'Christians rejoice . . .' blared the band.

Yes, even here! And Martine found herself squashed against Willy's chest, their bodies soldered together from top to toe, their mouths shamefully glued to one another.

'Dirty swine!'

Big Jeanne advanced towards them, her voice loud and vulgar, gesturing like a disjointed marionette.

'Not going to leave anything for the rest of us, then?'

Then, raising her voice:

'You, my girl, you could leave me some room!'

They still did not move and, seizing Martine by the shoulder, she pulled her away.

'Don't you understand, you little tart? Do you think he is yours alone, your Willy? What if I was jealous?'

People were listening, looking at them from the other tables.

'I haven't said anything till now. I've let you go because I'm a kind person. But that man there is mine ...'

'What's she saying?' asked the girl, surprised.

Willy vainly tried to push her aside.

'What am I saying? What am I saying? I'm saying you're a dirty whore and you've pinched him. I'm saying that I'm not having it and I'm going to smash your face in. I'm saying ... Well, take that for a start ... And that ... ! And that too ... !'

She was really going for it, hitting, scratching, pulling her hair as hard as she could, while they tried in vain to separate them.

She was strong as a man, Big Jeanne.

'Ah, you've treated me like—we know what ...! Aha, if you're looking for trouble ...'

Martine defended herself as well as she could, dug her nails into her back, even sank her little teeth into the hand pinching her ear.

'Come now ladies, gentlemen ...'

And always there was the shrill voice of Jeanne, who managed to push the table over. Glasses and bottles came crashing down. Women moved away, with a shriek, from the battle zone, while Big Jeanne finally succeeded in getting the girl on to the floor by tripping her up.

'Aha, if you're looking for me, well here I am!' They were on the floor with their arms around each other, with drops of blood on them from the shards of glass.

'Christians Rejoice' was being played at full blast to drown out their shouts. People carried on singing. And then the door opened. Two policemen with bicycles came in and went straight over to the two combatants.

Not too carefully, they poked them with the toes of their shoes.

'Up you get!'

'This whore ...'

'Be quiet, save your explanations for the police station.'

The men, Willy and friend, had vanished.

'Follow us.'

'But...' protested Martine.

'That'll do. No excuses!'

Big Jeanne turned round to get her hat, which she had lost in the fight. On the pavement she shouted to the waiter:

'Put my hat on one side, Jean. I'll come and get it tomorrow. It's almost new.'

'If you don't shut up...!' threatened one of the policemen, brandishing his handcuffs.

'Okay, cock! We'll be good little girls!'

Martine stumbled. And then was suddenly sick. They had to stop in a dark corner to let her vomit at the bottom of a wall on which was written 'No urinating here' in big white letters.

She was crying, a mixture of sobs and hiccups.

'I don't know what came over her. We were having such a nice time...'

'I bet!'

'I'd like a glass of water.'

'You'll get one at the station.'

It wasn't far, Rue de l'Étoile. And in fact Lognon, the surly inspector, was still on duty. His glasses were perched on his nose. He must have been in the middle of drawing up his report on the death of the Russian. He recognized Jeanne, and the other girl, and looked at each of them without comprehending what was going on.

'Did you know one another?'

'You could say that, mate!'

'You're pissed as a newt,' he told Jeanne. 'As for the other girl...'

One of the policemen explained:

'They were both on the floor, at the *Monico*, tearing each other's hair out.'

'Monsieur,' Martine tried to protest.

'That's enough! Put her in the cell while we wait for transport.'

There were men along one side, not many, old tramps mostly, and women on the other, at the back, separated by a lattice barrier. Benches along the walls. A little flower-seller in tears.

'What've you been up to?'

'They found coke in my flowers. It's not my fault...'

'Really!'

'Who's that one over there?'

'A slug.'

'A what?'

'A slug. Don't bother your head about it. Look! she's starting to throw up again. It's going to stink in here if the black maria's late.'

There were more than a hundred of them at three in the morning on the Quai de l'Horloge, at the police station, still the men on one side and the women on the other.

No doubt in thousands of houses they were still dancing in front of the Christmas trees. They'd have indigestion from the turkey, the foie gras, and the pudding. The restaurants and cafés wouldn't close till dawn.

'Don't you understand yet you little idiot?'

Martine was lying like a retriever on a bench as shiny with use as a church pew. She was still poorly, her face drawn, her eyes vague, her lips puffed out in a pout.

'I don't know what I've done to you.'

'You haven't done anything, slug.'

'You're a . . .'

'Ssh, don't say that word here, or you might get laid into by dozens of them.'

'I hate you.'

'That's probably true. Nevertheless you'd look a right ninny at this time of night in a hotel room in Rue Brey!'

You felt the girl was making an effort to understand.

'Don't bother your little head! But believe me when I tell you, you are okay here, even if it's not comfortable and doesn't smell too good. At eight o'clock the police chief will give the telling-off you deserve and you can get the metro for Place des Ternes. I'm sure they'll make me have a check-up and no doubt take away my licence for a week.'

'I don't get it.'

'For heaven's sake! Do you think it would have been any fun with that pig, and it being Christmas night and all? Eh? You would have been proud of your Willy the next morning! Do you think people weren't disgusted when you were snoring on the chest of that thug? Now at least you've got another chance. You can thank the Russian for that, see!'

'Why?'

'I dunno. Just a thought. First, it's because of him that I didn't go home. Then it may be because he made me want to play Father Christmas once in my life... Shove over, now, make space for me...'

Then, half-asleep:

'Suppose everybody played Father Christmas once in their lives...'

Her voice became dreamier as sleep began to get the better of her.

'Suppose, as I was saying . . . just once . . . with all the people who live on earth . . .'

Finally, with a grunt, her head on Martine's thigh, which she was using for a pillow, she said:

'And try not to wriggle all the time.'

Romance in the Metro

Claude Dufresne

Leaving home at 8.03, Hilaire Robichon reached the Porte de Vincennes metro at 8.12 precisely. Every morning for the last twenty-three years, Saturdays and Sundays excepted, he arrived there at the same time, at the same metro station. Time to buy his paper, get his weekly pass punched and reach the platform, and catch the 8.14 every morning, which set him down at Concorde exactly thirty-one minutes later. And this had been happening for nearly a quarter of a century, from the day he had started as an accountant at the Ministry of the Marine. For almost a quarter of a century he had crossed the Rue de Rivoli at 8.46 at the same pace, reached the ministry at 8.49, arrived on the third floor at 8.51, gone into the cloakroom and come out again at 8.54, greeted his colleague Mlle Dubillard and enquired after the health of her cats, which took him two minutes, and, taking the long corridor which led to his office, was at his desk by 8.58, that is, with the two minutes to spare every scrupulous employee owes it to himself to observe.

Never, in twenty-three years of good and faithful service, had the smallest hitch, the tiniest unexpected event, crept into Hilaire Robichon's timetable. He would not have been able to cope with it, in any case. For away from the ministry, in his private life, he observed the same punctuality. Whether it was the time he took his meals, went to bed, or read a book, everything was carefully regulated, measured out, compartmentalized in Hilaire Robichon's existence. Chance, the Unforeseen, Impulse—these were meaningless words to him. And, as he was pushing forty-seven, there was no reason why this should change now. He must have been young once, like everyone else, but it was so long ago he couldn't remember. Moreover, an unprepossessing face, average height, and crippling shyness had sheltered him from any excitement. Never a brilliant scholar, when his studies were over he had lived with his mother, who seemed the very incarnation of the speaking clock. For years she had spoken to her son only to remind him that he had one minute to wash his hands before sitting down to a meal, a quarter of an hour to do the dishes, and half an hour to mend the old radio that broke down three times a week. When, abruptly, this lady ceased to be, carried off by a pneumonia that also had not one moment to lose, it never crossed Hilaire's mind to adjust his timetable.

Only love might have made a splash of colour in this dull existence, but as to that, Hilaire's physical appearance had spared him the torments of passion. As far as love affairs were concerned, Hilaire had known only one, of which his colleague Mlle Dubillard had been the happy beneficiary. And even then Mlle Dubillard had had to make the first and even the second moves! One day she had suggested that he come and see her darling little pussy-cats, whose exploits nourished her daily conversation. Not without some hesitation, Hilaire had accepted and, arranging the meeting three weeks in advance, had gone to Mlle Dubillard's place one Sunday. But once he was settled with a cup of tea and biscuits in front of him he could not help noticing that the feline species occupied only a secondary place in Mlle Dubillard's need for affection. The old maid was concealing a passionate nature which Aphrodite herself might have envied. Perhaps for

Hilaire it was the opportunity to escape his fate. But that was exactly what he did not want, at any price. He continued to show he was the same time-keeping bureaucrat in matters of love as he was in everything else. Discouraged, Mlle Dubillard had returned to her cats and Hilaire had gone back with some relief to his comfortable habits. However, gentleman that he was, he gave up two minutes of his time every morning to talk to Mlle Dubillard about her cats. It was his way of demonstrating to her that she had not been dealing with a disagreeable kind of person.

This morning then, as every morning, he had sat down in a carriage on the Vincennes—Neuilly line, without paying any attention to the faces of the other travellers. So he had not noticed that a most beautiful creature was following close on his heels and had got into the same carriage. For she really was the woman of one's dreams. Her slim figure, her elegance, her sparkling green eyes, the gold of her hair would have unleashed a riot in a Trappist monastery. But Hilaire, not having noticed any human being for a very long time, did not notice her, woman of one's dreams or not. Yet she sat down right opposite him, and the unaccustomed appearance of this young woman, one obviously meant to be travelling around in a Rolls, should have, at the very least, occasioned a glimmer of surprise on Hilaire's face. But he was lost, as usual, in his newspaper, and he paid not the least bit of attention to the unknown beauty.

Hilaire Robichon brought to the perusal of his newspaper the care he took in performing every little action, reading it from cover to cover, from the small ads to the bank rates. Thus it was at Nation station that he attacked its second page. At Bastille he turned the third page. At that moment the mysterious woman coughed and came to sit next to Hilaire. Automatically he raised his eyes and lowered them at once to his newspaper, not looking longer at his neighbour than if she had been an old man with a pot-belly. Three more stations went past in this manner. At Châtelet the young woman coughed again, but there was still no reaction from Hilaire. He was on page 6 of his newspaper, and the mysterious woman, with all her throat-clearing, must have had no saliva left. It was then she decided to attack. In a beautiful, grave, and sensual voice such as the Sirens must have had, she said to Hilaire: 'Excuse me, Monsieur, could you tell me which station I have to change at to get to Palais Royal?'

Hilaire did not answer immediately, but turned round to see who his neighbour was addressing. The idea that a woman might speak to him did not enter his head. However, when the mysterious woman, with a smile that would have made Sophia Loren's fade in comparison, repeated her question, Hilaire had to bow before the evidence: it was him she meant. Then all at once he saw how beautiful the young woman was, and this realization literally took his breath away. After a violent effort he nevertheless managed to stutter: 'The next one, Madame.'

The mysterious woman then replied, to his utter amazement:

'And where are you getting off?'

'Concorde, of course,' he answered, as if the entire world must know that in twenty-three years he had never got off anywhere else.

But the mysterious woman seemed completely un-abashed, and calmly announced:

'In that case I shall get off at Concorde too.'

Poor Hilaire then turned all the colours of the rainbow. But what showed in his face was nothing compared with the terrible anxiety that tightened around his heart. Why was this woman changing her destination? How was it possible to decide to get off at Concorde when you were going to Palais Royal? More-over, had she been less beautiful Hilaire would have been less afraid, but from his reading, he had known for a long time that such creatures looking like vamps were extremely dangerous. While he was turning over these scariest of thoughts in his head, Concorde station appeared and Hilaire leaped from his seat. For the first time in twenty-three years he had almost gone past his stop. He hurried to the exit, but when he looked behind he was stricken with panic: the young woman had followed him. Almost at a run, Hilaire crossed the Rue de Rivoli. In his turmoil he realized he had forgotten to cross at the crossing. But he didn't have time for lengthy self-recriminations on this severe failure on his part, for the young woman took him by the arm and asked:

'Where are you off to in such a hurry?'

'To the Ministry of the Marine, I'm a civil servant,' Hilaire heard himself reply, as if in a bad dream.

The unknown woman's reply increased his worries a hundredfold:

'No question of going to the Ministry today! Follow me!'

Gathering all his remaining strength, Hilaire still had enough left to protest: 'But what will Monsieur Chalabar, my office manager, say?' It was obvious that the mysterious woman cared as much about Monsieur Chalabar as about her first pair of false eyelashes. She was already briskly hailing a taxi and ushering Hilaire, now at the end of his tether, into it. Like a ship's captain vanquished by the storm, he decided at that point to give himself up entirely to a fate stronger than him.

From then on, events for Hilaire took on the blurry outlines of a dream. The taxi set them down on the Avenue George V outside a luxury hotel which, still propelled forward by the young woman, Hilaire entered as though sleepwalking. On the way there the unknown woman had told him her name was Gladys de Saint-Foix and that she belonged to an important public-relations organization. But when Hilaire asked her why she was interested in a humble accountant at the Ministry of the Marine, she smiled her ravishing and enigmatic smile and replied, modestly lowering her eyes: 'One should never ask a woman why she shows an interest in a man.'

This answer threw Hilaire into an abyss of perplexity. Was it possible that he, Hilaire Robichon, had attracted this powerful beauty-queen?

The question so preoccupied him that he followed Gladys around like an automaton for the rest of the morning. After a breakfast of the kind only eaten in American movies, there was a ride in the Bois de Boulogne in a Rolls that was also straight out of a Hollywood props room; after that, a visit to a famous tailor, and thence to an elegant shirtmaker's, from where Hilaire emerged transformed from head to toe. During these successive operations Gladys waxed more and more eloquent, but Hilaire did not even hear her. A new thought was obsessing him: 'It's a nightmare, I'm going to wake up!'

But he didn't. Or rather, he only woke up during lunch at Maxim's, when he noticed Monsieur Chalabar coming out of the Ministry on his way to the canteen. A cold sweat broke out over Hilaire's spine:

'My office manager... Monsieur Chalabar,' he muttered in torment.

But Monsieur Chalabar certainly did not have the honour of impressing Gladys:

'Monsieur Chalabar can go to hell,' she decreed, with a saucy look.

This sentence, which even that morning would have plunged Hilaire into a state of appalled terror, in one instant set him free from the taboos that had governed his life till then. This model civil servant who respected his superiors from the very core of his being forswore twenty-three years of bowing and scraping with that one magic little phrase. For the first time in his life he dared raise his voice and shout: 'Yes, Monsieur Chalabar can go to hell!'

He had spoken so loudly that several people turned round, but Hilaire didn't care. In one instant he had become a different man. So he went along with Gladys's various caprices with utter sang-froid. From then on he felt as if he were the one doing the leading. He had made a conquest of a woman as rich as she was beautiful, and that thought, far from driving him mad, plunged him into the most delightful euphoria. He felt capable of anything, and when Gladys suggested they should go to a *thé dansant*, he who had never dared even to take part in the dances put on by the local parish priest, did not hesitate for one second, but threw himself on to the dance-floor with the calm confidence of someone used to frequenting Régine's.

As time went by he felt he was gaining ground in Gladys's affections. So when, at the end of the day, she suggested going back to the hotel to change for dinner, he didn't doubt for a second that his moment of glory had arrived. The irresistible passion that he had engendered in the young woman was about to be consummated.

Two adjoining suites had been reserved in the big hotel on the Avenue George V. In his, Hilaire found a dinner-jacket of elegant cut which he put on with the natural gestures of the man of the world that he had now become. Then, knocking on Gladys's door, he did not even wait to be invited in. The young woman seemed a little surprised. 'I'm not quite ready,' she said, with a little embarrassed smile.

Clearly, Hilaire had no experience of such situations. So he had to have recourse to his memory of a recent American series on television which portrayed the exploits of an out-and-out seducer. Hilaire replied, just as he had seen the hero of the adventure do, with imperturbable sang-froid: 'No problem, Baby, we got our whole life ahead of us,' and matched his action to his words. Alas, we must assume that Gladys had never seen the series in question, for instead of fluttering her eyelids and falling into his arms, she managed to dodge deftly out of the way and Hilaire found himself flat on his stomach on the carpet. As if nothing had happened, Gladys helped him to regain a vertical position and said gaily: 'Let's hurry or we shall be late for the surprise...'

Surprise? Hilaire had just had one, rather a nasty one. His shoulders arched, his eyes clouded over, and suddenly he was again the timid little model employee he had always been. So, meekly, he allowed himself to be led by Gladys in the direction of that famous restaurant on the banks of the Seine where, apparently, they were expected. For him at present the dream was over, even if on the surface it seemed to be continuing.

Meanwhile, the Rolls had set them down in front of the restaurant, and a bellboy had whisked them into a special room where a dozen extremely distinguished gentlemen were waiting for them with evident impatience. And suddenly Hilaire was stunned: amongst the guests was Monsieur Chalabar... A smiling Monsieur Chalabar, who came towards Hilaire and, instead of treating him like a dog, as he usually did, shook his hand cordially and said: 'My dear Robichon, it's an honour which we all share in at the Ministry. That's why I was only too glad to accept the invitation from these gentlemen.'

It was then that Hilaire noticed the streamer strung across the back of the room. There were only a few words on it, but they were enough to jolt him back into reality: 'Welcome to the billionth traveller on the Metropolitan!'

Hilaire turned to Gladys. She seemed suddenly not to be there. She would not meet Hilaire's eye. Her beauty had dimmed. Hilaire moved next to her and murmured under his breath: 'You should have told me. You shouldn't have made a fool of me.'

A little tear appeared in the corner of Gladys's pretty eye, and in a slightly choked voice she replied: 'I wanted you to have one day of real happiness in your life.' But already an important gentleman was catching hold of Hilaire's arm and declaring, with obvious satisfaction: 'Dear Monsieur Robichon, this was a present from the RATP to its billionth traveller: however, we have still something else for you: a pass which gives you one year's free travel on the metro...'

But the pass the important gentleman was holding out to Hilaire remained suspended in his fingers, while Hilaire said, gently but firmly: 'It is of no use, Monsieur. Never in my life shall I take the metro again.'

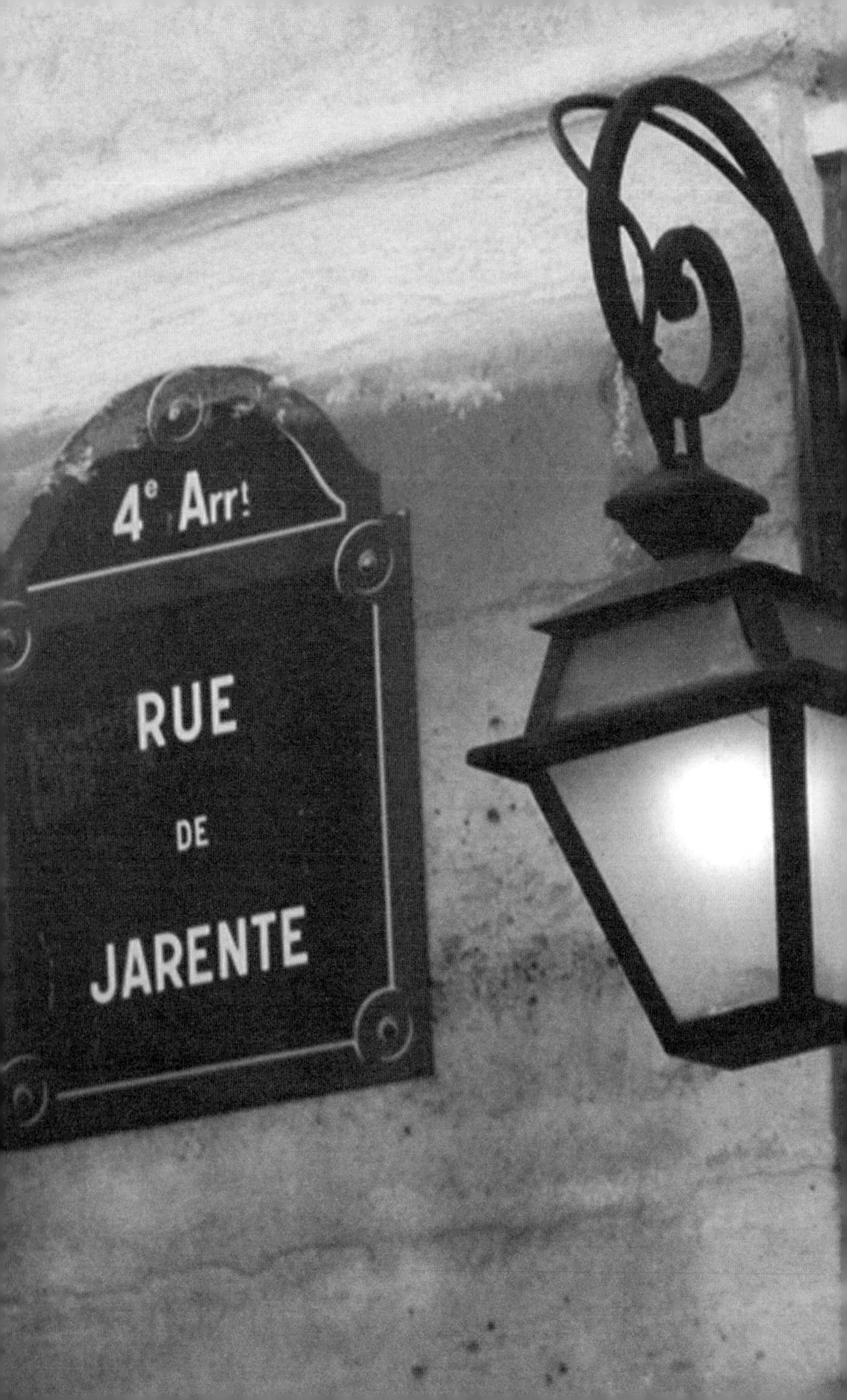
4e Arrt
RUE
DE
JARENTE

The Neighbour in the Rue de Jarente

Cyrille Fleischman

Ten years ago—yes, ten years already, 1947 to be precise—the agency promised to replace the light in the corridor with something other than a night-light like the ones they have in mortuaries.

No doubt the owner of the flats either didn't take any notice of the agency or else didn't remember, but every time Arthur Klergz went back home to the Rue de Jarente he nearly broke his leg in this dimly lit passageway. He knew there was a step in a certain place, but it was dark in that exact spot and he stumbled every time.

There seemed no future in remaining as tenants in such an old house, so Klergz and his wife, who kept a little shop not far from the Saint-Paul metro, borrowed what was necessary to buy a new flat. Since there was nothing modern available in that area they moved into the fourteenth arrondissement, while they carried on working in the fourth.

They were not very happy, however, in their newly built block of flats. The lifts were often broken, the concierges were not very nice, you had to change metros to get to Saint-Paul, and in addition to that, Klergz's wife died.

After the traditional thirty days mourning, Arthur Klergz, who found his fourteenth arrondissement apartment too big and gloomy, just out of curiosity telephoned the agency that managed the flat where he had lived before. He learned that a small flat had fallen vacant on the second floor in his old place in the Rue de Jarente. He asked if the light in the hallway had been replaced and the man told him no, but he would see to it.

That was how it came about that Klergz sold his apartment in the fourteenth arrondissement, paid off the loan, put what little remained in the savings bank in Rue Saint-Antoine and relocated to the Rue de Jarente.

The first evening when he went back home after supper with his brother-in-law who lived in the Rue de Turenne, he noticed that the light in the hallway was not really any better. True, the original bulb had been replaced by a neon strip. But unfortunately it was a neon strip with such a time delay that it didn't begin to light the hall till about a year after you had pressed the button. Klergz therefore had ample time to curse the man, before falling in the spot where he had all but forgotten there was a hidden step.

No real harm was done, but at that moment another tenant arrived, key in hand.

Irina S. had moved into the Rue de Jarente a little while before, after her divorce. Perhaps it was to ward off her fright at seeing a shape moving on the floor, or perhaps because she was a woman of the world and not the kind to recoil at the sight of a drunk or a satyr, but she gave the man crouching there a sharp little kick.

'*Sortez de là, vous!*'

Klergz got up, rubbing his back. The neon strip, not coming on properly but blinking a little, lit the hallway with a faint light.

She put her hand over her mouth:

'Oh I'm awfully sorry, I thought you were ...'

She was stammering at first:

'I thought you were...'

Then, not wanting to give offence, she said kindly:

'I thought you must be a cat.'

Klergz was still so shocked that all he could say was:

'Do you normally say "vous" to a cat?'

He rubbed his back again and explained:

'It's because of the light. I've told the manager a hundred times that you can't see a thing in this hall.'

'Yes I know,' she replied. 'I've hardly been living here two months—after my divorce, you know—but every week when I come back from the Saint-Paul cinema at night I notice it. I ought to buy a torch like the ones the usherettes have...'

She giggled loudly. Klergz laughed too. He took a closer look at her. She was pretty and friendly and she was young. She couldn't have been more than fifty. But because he had heard the word 'divorce', he assumed a sympathetic tone.

'Have you been...you and your husband...? It must be hard nowadays for a woman on her own. I've lost my wife as well. In the fourteenth arrondissement. The fourteenth, it wasn't like here...'

Irina did not quite understand all he was saying, but he meant well and she, too, found she liked him. He was young, he couldn't have been much above sixty.

'Do you live here?' she asked.

'Since *before* the war and except *during* the war. When we came back after, we moved to the fourteenth. And now I'm on my own and I'm here again. Well, you know, that's life, that's the way of it . . . Tell me,' he went on, 'may I offer you a cup of tea? I live on the second floor, the light here is so dim that we don't even want to be talking in the hallway.'

'A cup of tea at eleven o'clock at night? I wouldn't be able to sleep. Come to my room instead. I live on the third. I'll make some mint and lime-blossom. As long as mint doesn't keep you awake at night. Some people can't drink it.'

'No no, mint is excellent for the health,' Klergz said approvingly.

She put her hand on the banisters and began to climb the stairs, followed by Klergz. 'Mint is excellent. A good idea,' he repeated, holding on tight to the banisters.

'I think so too,' she said, turning round. 'Mixed with lime-blossom, it's good for the digestion. But some people can't take it at night.'

So they continued talking until they arrived at Irina's door.

Arthur Klergz wondered if he was not falling a little bit in love. All because of the manager, actually, and the light downstairs not working.

At any rate, he had rarely been so happy to talk to someone.

As if she had guessed his train of thought, Irina turned to him and said:

'Life is strange, isn't it?'

At that moment the door next to Irina's opened abruptly.

Wortavitch, a neighbour Klergz had known for a very long time, came out on to the landing in his dressing-gown.

'Is that you making that noise on the stairs? You're stopping me sleeping!'

He acknowledged Irina with a curt nod.

'I fell over just now,' Klergz explained, 'and this lady is going to make me some mint and lime-blossom tea so...'

Wortavitch slipped both hands into his dressing-gown pocket and gave a sarcastic laugh:

'Drink? When you've been hurt? Do you think that's such a great idea? If they end up taking you to casualty and you have to be operated on, do you imagine the surgeon would be pleased if you'd drunk something hot before the anaesthetic?'

'But I don't have to be operated on,' Klergz protested, taking a step back.

Wortavitch addressed the wall:

'Are you telling me, the brother of a doctor, who should or should not have an operation?'

He turned to Klergz, looking straight into his eyes:

'It's not up to you to decide. It's up to the surgeon. I forbid you to have a drink now. I'm a responsible neighbour, I am. Come in and I'll call the ambulance from here.'

'Don't worry about it,' trilled Irina. 'I shall just make him a small sweet tea and he will go to bed. Tomorrow he'll have forgotten all about it.'

That worked Wortavitch up even more. He addressed the other wall.

'A world full of irresponsible people! We are living in a world where even women who don't know the first thing about it have an opinion about injuries! Madame,' he said, speaking to her, 'Monsieur Klergz, who is a very old friend of mine, is my responsibility from this minute. It's up to me to take care of him. That's only natural is it not, when I was friends with his poor wife, whom everyone round here thought the world of, and whose funeral we attended?'

The evocation of his wife's memory made Klergz lose heart completely, and he threw a despairing look at Irina.

She gave him a little wave:

'I'm sorry, it's late, I shall say goodnight and go to bed.'

Wortavitch nodded at her, and pushed Klergz into his own flat.

He didn't call the doctor or the ambulance, but, being a chronic insomniac, he began talking about the agency, then about the war, then about his own life, then about his brother's, then about their father's in Russia before the Revolution. When, after some time, he saw that Klergz was no longer listening, he escorted him out on to the landing and advised him to go and see a doctor tomorrow. He slipped his brother's card into Klergz's jacket pocket and slammed the door behind him.

The light on the landing wasn't very good either. It suddenly went out and Klergz, who had to go down a floor in the dark, nearly slipped again. But his mind was on other things and, as he grabbed hold of the banisters, he was thinking he would probably never again have the luck to be helped by such a pretty woman.

Moreover, Irina S. moved out shortly after. Without leaving her new address.

As for Wortavitch, he lived in the block of flats for many years after that. A permanent reminder for Arthur Klergz that love was not made to blossom in the Rue de Jarente. Nor, perhaps, anywhere else in this world.

The Landlady
for Doctor Baraduc

Guy de Maupassant

In those days, said Georges Kervelen, I lived in a furnished house in Rue des Saints-Pères.

When my parents decided I should go to Paris to read law, there were long discussions to sort everything out. The price of my board and lodging had been fixed at 2,500 francs, but my poor mother was consumed by worries and voiced them to my father: 'If he were to throw away all his money and not eat properly, his health would be badly affected. You can never tell with these young people.'

So it was decided to find lodgings for me, some comfortable place that was not too expensive, and my family was to meet the cost directly, each month.

I'd never left Quimper before. I wanted everything people of my age want and I was disposed to enjoy life in all possible ways.

When asked for their advice, neighbours told them about a compatriot, a Mme Kergaran, who took in lodgers. So my father got in touch with this good lady by letter, and I duly arrived at her house one evening, accompanied by a trunk.

Mme Kergaran was about forty. She was a large woman, very large, spoke like a sergeant-major and resolved all questions briskly and conclusively. Her house, which was very narrow, had only one window on the street on each floor, and thus resembled a ladder with windows, or a slice of a house in between two others, like a sandwich.

The landlady lived on the first floor with her servant-girl; the cooking was done and meals eaten on the second; four lodgers from Brittany lodged on the third and fourth floor. I had the two rooms on the fifth.

A small dark staircase, winding up like a corkscrew, led to these two attic rooms. Every day and all day Mme Kergaran went up and down the spiral staircase, busying herself in this chest of drawers of a lodging-house like a captain on board ship. Ten times a day she would come roaring and fussing into each flat, to cast her eye over everything, check if the beds were properly made, the clothes properly brushed, and the servant-girl's chores properly done. In brief, she looked after her lodgers like a mother, or better than a mother.

I had soon made the acquaintance of my four compatriots. Two were studying medicine, and the other two law, but they all were under the despotic yoke of the landlady. They were afraid of her, as a poacher is afraid of a gamekeeper.

As for me, I immediately felt the need to be independent, for I am one of nature's rebels. I straightaway declared that I wished to come back at a time that suited me, for Mme Kergaran had imposed a midnight curfew. At this demand she fixed her sharp eyes upon me for a few seconds and declared:

'That's not possible. I cannot allow Annette to be wakened at all hours. You've no business to be out after a certain time.'

I replied firmly: 'According to the law, Madame, you have to let me in at any time. If you refuse I shall inform the police and go and put up in a hotel at your expense, as I am entitled to do. Then you will be obliged to let me in or get rid of me. You give me a key or I leave. You choose.'

I was laughing in her face as I set out these conditions. After a last look of stunned surprise she wanted to start negotiations, but I was obdurate and she gave in. We came to an agreement that I would come and go as I pleased on the strict understanding that no one else should know about it.

My forceful attitude had a salutary effect upon her, and after that she made a real favourite of me. She looked after me, waited on me, did little favours, and displayed even a brusque tenderness towards me to which I was not in the least averse. Sometimes when I was feeling particularly playful I gave her an unexpected kiss, for no reason except to get the hard slap she administered immediately after. When I managed to duck quickly enough, her hand whizzed past me in mid-flight with the speed of a bullet, and I ran off, laughing like a mad thing, with her shouting: 'Ah, you little devil, I'll get my own back!'

We had become friends.

But then I made the acquaintance, in the street, of a girl who worked in a shop.

You know what these Paris affairs are like. One day on the way to college, you meet a bare-headed girl, walking arm-in-arm with her girlfriend before going back to work. You exchange looks, and get that little shudder that comes when some women look at you. It's one of the joys of life, this instant physical sympathy you have when you meet someone, the light, subtle attraction you feel suddenly for a person born to please you and be loved in return. A lot or a little, does it matter? It's natural that she answers the secret desire for love in you. From the first time you set eyes on that face, that mouth, that hair, that smile, her charms suffuse you with a sweet, delicious sensation; a sense of well-being comes over you, and a confused desire, impelling you towards this unknown woman, is suddenly born. You seem to be answering a call in her, an attraction which requires an answer; you feel you have known her a long time, that you have seen her before, that you know what she is thinking.

The next day, at the same time, you go down the same street. You see her again. Then you go back the following day, and again the day after that. Finally you speak. And the affair runs its course, as predictable as a sickness.

So, after three weeks, Emma and I had entered the period that precedes the fall. Her fall would have happened even sooner had I known how to bring it about. My girlfriend lived with her parents and refused point blank to cross the threshold of a *hotel de passe*. I racked my brains to find some means, some ruse, or opportunity. In the end I resorted to the desperate remedy of getting her to come up to my room one evening at about eleven, on the pretext of a cup of tea. Mme

Kergaran went to bed each night at ten. Therefore
I could get in with my key without making a noise or
arousing suspicion. We would go down again the same
way after an hour or two.

Emma, after refusing once or twice, agreed.

I had a bad day. I was uneasy. I feared complica-
tions, a catastrophe, some terrible scandal. Evening
came. I went out to a café where I drank two cups of
coffee and four or five small glasses, to give me
strength. Then I went for a walk on the Boulevard
Saint Michel. I heard it strike ten, ten-thirty. I made
my way slowly to where we were going to meet. She was
already there, waiting. She took hold of my arm in a
flirtatious manner and we made our way slowly towards my house. As we got nearer the door, my anxiety
increased. I thought: 'I hope Mme Kervalan is in bed.'

I said to Emma two or three times: 'Whatever you
do, don't make a noise on the stairs.'

She began to laugh: 'Are you scared someone will
hear us?'

'No, but I don't want to wake up my neighbour who
is very ill.'

We've reached Rue des Saints-Pères. I approach my
lodgings with the same apprehension I get when I go to
the dentist. All the windows are in darkness. No doubt

everyone is asleep. I breathe again. I open the door, cautious as a burglar. I usher in my companion, then shut the door behind me and climb the stairs on tiptoe, holding my breath and striking matches to light the way so that my girl doesn't fall over.

As we pass the landlady's room I can feel my heart thumping faster. Finally we reach the second floor, then the third, then the fifth. I enter my room. We've made it!

I only dared speak in low tones, however, and I took off my boots so as not to make a noise. Tea, made on a spirit-lamp, was drunk on the corner of my chest of drawers. Then I was in a hurry...a great hurry...and gradually, like in a game, I took my girl's clothes off, one by one, with her yielding then resisting, blushing, embarrassed, and still putting off the final, delicious moment.

She had nothing on but a short white petticoat, when suddenly my door flew open and Mme Kergaran appeared, candle in hand, in exactly the same state of undress as Emma.

I had leapt away from her and was standing there aghast, looking at the two women who were staring at each other. Whatever was going to happen?

The landlady pronounced, in a disdainful and unfamiliar voice: 'I want no girls in my house, Monsieur Kervelen.'

I stammered: 'But Madame Kergaran, this young lady is only a friend. She came up for a cup of tea.'

The plump woman replied: 'You don't strip to your petticoat to drink a cup of tea. Have this person leave immediately.'

Emma, appalled, was beginning to cry and hid her face in her skirt. I lost my head, not knowing what to do or say. The landlady added, with an authority that brooked no resistance: 'Help this young lady dress and see her home immediately.'

There was nothing else for it, that was certain, so I picked up her dress that had fallen around her, like a burst balloon, on the wooden floor, then drew it over the girl's head, and had a great deal of trouble trying to hook and fasten it. She helped me, still in tears, distressed and hurried, making all sorts of mistakes, unable to find either laces or buttonholes; and the impassive Mme Kergaran stood there, candle in hand, shining her light in the grim attitude of one dispensing justice.

Emma's movements were now even faster, she flung on her clothes with frantic gestures, tied, fastened, laced, did herself up in a frenzy, driven by the powerful need to escape; and without even buttoning up her boots, she ran out in front of the landlady and rushed downstairs. I followed her in my slippers, only half-clothed myself, saying again and again: 'Mademoiselle, listen, Mademoiselle.'

I knew I should say something to her, but didn't know what. I caught her up just at the front door, and tried to take hold of her arm, but she pushed me back violently, stammering in a low, nervous voice: 'Let me go, let me go, don't touch me.'

And she ran off into the road, slamming the door behind her.

I turned round. Mme Kergaran had remained upstairs on the first floor and I went slowly up again, expecting and prepared for whatever was coming.

The landlady's door was open. In a grave voice she called me in: 'I need to speak to you, Monsieur Kervelen.'

Head bowed, I passed in front of her. She placed her candlestick on the mantelpiece then, with arms crossed on her formidable bosom, which was scantily covered by a fine white camisole:

'So, Monsieur Kervelen, you take my house for a bawdy house!'

I was not pleased with myself. I mumbled: 'Of course not, Madame Kergaran. Don't be cross now, you know what young men are like.'

She answered:

'I know I don't want *people* in my house, do you understand? I know I wish to keep a respectable house, and to keep up the reputation of my house, do you understand? I know...'

She went on for at least twenty minutes, alternately reasoning and expressing indignation, overwhelming me with talk of the honour of her *house*, assaulting me with repeated and bitter recriminations.

Man is a strange animal. Instead of listening to her, I just looked at her. I didn't hear another word, not one word. This amazon had a superb bosom, firm, plump, and white, a little too big perhaps, but so tempting as to send a shiver down your spine. Truly, I would never have supposed that such things existed under the landlady's woollen dress. Without any clothes on she seemed ten years younger. And now I was feeling very strange, very...What should I say...disturbed. In front of her I was suddenly in the same state...that I had been in and had been interrupted in a quarter of an hour earlier in my bedroom.

And, behind her, over there in the alcove, I looked at her bed. It was uncovered, the sheet was crumpled, and the dip in the bedclothes testified to the weight of the body that had lain there. And I thought it must be very nice and warm in there, warmer than in any other bed. Why warmer? I don't know, undoubtedly because of the opulence of the flesh which had been lying there.

Is there anything more troubling and delightful than a rumpled bed? The sight of that one, even at a distance went to my head, made my flesh tingle.

She was still talking, but more softly now, as if she were a frank, well-meaning friend only seeking to forgive.

I stammered: 'Come now, come now, Madame Kergaran, come now.' And as she had fallen silent to let me reply, I seized her in my arms and started to kiss her, again and again, like one desperate, like a man who has been waiting for it for a long time.

She turned her face away, fending me off, but without becoming too angry, repeating her usual automatic phrase: 'Oh the devil, the devil, the de...'

She could not finish, for, with a huge effort, I had picked her up and carried her across, holding her tight in my arms. Suddenly I was strong as an ox!

I met the edge of the bed, and fell upon it without letting her go...

It was indeed nice and warm in her bed.

An hour later and the candle extinguished, the landlady got up to light the other one. And as she slipped back in bed with me, burying her plump, strong legs beneath the sheets, she uttered, in tender tones that were perhaps both satisfied and grateful: 'Oh the little devil, the little devil...!'

La Butte Montmartre

Gérard de Nerval

It's very hard finding somewhere to live in Paris.—I've never felt this more than during the last two months. Returning from Germany, after a brief stay in a villa out of town, I looked for lodgings more secure than my previous places, one of which was in the Place du Louvre and the other in the Rue du Mail.—I mention only those within the last six years.—Evicted from the first with twenty francs in compensation, which, I don't know why, I neglected to collect from the Municipality, I found in the second something you scarcely find at all in the centre of Paris nowadays: a view over two or three trees with a certain amount of space around them, so that you could breathe and at the same time refresh the mind by looking at something other than a chequerboard of black windows where only very rarely does a pretty face appear.—

I respect my neighbours' privacy. I am not one for peering through a telescope at the curves of a woman getting ready for bed or for spying with the naked eye on the incidents and accidents of married life in their particular silhouettes.—I prefer a horizon 'made to delight the eyes', as Fénelon might say, where you may enjoy sunrise or sunset, but the former especially. Sunsets I need not worry about: I am certain to encounter them anywhere but at home. Sunrise is a different matter: I like to watch the sun making angles on the walls and to listen to the twitterings of birds outside, and be they only common sparrows ... Grétry offered a louis to hear the singing of a *chanterelle*, I'd give twenty francs for a blackbird—the twenty francs the Municipality of Paris still owes me!

I have lived a good deal in Montmartre. The air is very pure up there, the views are varied, and the horizons are magnificent, whether, 'having been virtuous you like to watch day dawn', a very beautiful sight on the Paris side, or whether, your tastes being less simple, you prefer the crimsons of sunset and the tatters of floating cloud in scenes of battle and transfiguration over the great cemetery between the arch of Étoile and the bluish hills that extend from Argenteuil to Pontoise.—New houses are forever advancing like the diluvian sea that washed against the slopes of the ancient mountain and little by little entered the last hiding-places of the unshapely monsters since put back together again by Cuvier.—Assaulted on one side by the Rue de l'Empereur and on the other by the civic quarter which is sapping the rough gradients and flattening the heights of the Paris slope, the old Hill of Mars will soon go the way of the Butte des Moulins, which in the last century faced up to the world hardly less proudly.— But we do still have a certain number of eminences enclosed by thick green hedges that the berberis adorns in season with its purple flowers and its crimson berries. There are windmills, taverns and bowers, Elysian haunts and silent little alleyways going in among cottages, barns, and luxuriant gardens, level green spaces curtailed by precipices where springs filter through the clay and make, in time, small verdant islands that frolicking goats frequent to graze on the acanthus hanging from the rocks. Little girls with proud looks and the feet of mountaineers keep an eye on them whilst playing their own games. You will even find a vineyard here, the last of the famous Montmartre name that in Roman times competed with Argenteuil and Suresnes. Every year this humble patch loses another row of its stunted vines: they tumble into a quarry.—Ten years ago I could have bought it for 3,000 francs. They are asking 30,000 for it now. It has the finest view in all the environs of Paris.

What attracted me in this small space sheltered by the great trees of the Château des Brouillards was first that remnant of a vineyard linked to the memory of Saint Denis who, in the opinion of the philosophers, was perhaps a second Bacchus (Dionysus) and who had three bodies, one of which was buried in Montmartre, the second in Ratisbon, and the third in Corinth.—And then the closeness of the watering-place that is lively in the evening with the spectacle of horses and dogs being bathed, and next to it a well built in antique style where the washer-girls gossip and sing as in one of the early chapters of *Werther*. With a bas-relief dedicated to Diana and perhaps a couple of naiads sculpted half-emergent, there, shaded by the old limes that overhang this monument, you would have an admirable retreat, entirely quiet at times, reminiscent of certain studies of the Roman *campagna*. Higher up, you can make out the windings of the Rue des Brouillards which descends towards the Chemin des Boeufs, then the garden of Gaucher's restaurant with its kiosks, lanterns, and painted statues.—The plain of Saint-Denis is admirably well delineated, and hour by hour along its borders the slopes of Saint-Ouen and Montmorency change their appearance under the moving sun and clouds. To the right there is a row of houses, most of them shut up because of cracks in the walls. It is this that guarantees the relative solitude of the place: for the horses and cattle that pass, and even the washer-women, will not disturb a thinker in his thoughts but will be part of them.—Town life itself, its common-place interests and dealings, prompt him to take him-self as far away as possible from the great centres of activity.

To the left there are large tracts of land, now cover-ing the site of a quarry that has fallen in, which have been leased by the commune to hard-working men who have quite transformed them. They have planted trees and made plots for potatoes and beet where formerly the mountain asparagus displayed its green fronds laced with red pearls.

You go down the track and turn left. Two or three green hills have survived here, cut into by a road which, further on, fills in some deep gullies and one day will most likely connect with the Rue de l'Empereur at a point between the hillocks and the cemetery. There you come upon a hamlet which already feels very much like the country. Three years ago it had an unhealthy pow-der-works, but that was discontinued and nowadays they work with leftovers from stearin candle factories.—How many artists denied the *Prix de Rome* have come here to study the *campagna* and the appearance of the Pontine Marshes! There really is still a marsh, lively with ducks, goslings, and hens. And it is no rare thing either hereabouts to see picturesque rags on the shoulders of workers.

The hills, split open in places, show the piling up of the land on old quarries. But nothing is lovelier than the appearance of the great hill when the sun illuminates its earth of red ochre veined with lime and clay, its denuded rocks, and some still quite dense copses of trees with paths and gullies winding through them. Most of the land and the few houses of this little valley have elderly owners who are banking on the difficulties Parisians face in building new homes, and on the likelihood that houses in the Montmartre quarter will, when the time comes, invade the Saint-Denis plain. These owners are a sluice-gate holding back the flood. When it opens their land will be expensive.—All the greater my regret that ten years ago I let slip the chance of giving 3,000 francs for Montmartre's last vineyard.

But no more of that. I shall never be a property-owner. And yet how often on the eighth or the fifteenth of every quarter (near Paris at least) I have sung Monsieur Vautour's refrain:

> When you can't pay the rent
> What you want is a house of your own!

Such an airy thing I'd have built on that vineyard...
A small villa in the style of Pompeii with an *impluvium*
and a *cella*, something like the House of the Tragic
Poet. My poor friend Laviron, dead since on the walls
of Rome, had drawn me the plan of it.—But strictly
speaking, there are no property-owners on the hills of
Montmartre. You cannot legally establish a property on
ground undermined by caverns within whose confines
there is a population of mammoths and mastodons.
The commune will grant a right of possession which
lapses after one hundred years...We have camped like
the Turks; and surely no doctrine, however advanced,
would contest such a transitory right to an inheritance
that will not last.

Notes on the Paris Metro

Gare du Nord

The station most familiar to travellers from Britain is the third busiest in the world, with around 180 million passengers a year passing through it. Inaugurated in 1846, it was soon too small to cope with the traffic and was partially demolished in 1860, when the façade was moved to Lille. It was rebuilt by Jacques Hittorff between 1861 and 1864, and then in 1889 the interior was again rebuilt. The sculpture on the façade described by Jacques Réda represents the cities, both national and international, served by the company. Each sculpture is by a different artist. In 1906 it was connected to the first metro line, Line 4. Take this line to reach the next metro station, **Saint-Michel**.

Saint-Michel

Place Saint-Michel in the heart of the Latin Quarter was the site of many demonstrations and uprisings, including the famous ones in May 1968. Perhaps the most touristic area of Paris, it is still one of the most beautiful. A short walk along the Seine towards Notre Dame takes you to the ancient church of Saint-Julien-le-Pauvre described by Julien Green, passing on your way the famous bookshop Shakespeare & Company, whose original shop was founded by Sylvia Beach in 1919. Return to **Saint-Michel** metro, take Line 4 and change at **Châtelet**, or walk across the river past Notre Dame to **Châtelet** and take line 11 for **Belleville**.

Belleville

The metro is on the site of the Barrière de Belleville, one of the many places in the Paris fortifications where taxes were collected until the French Revolution. The Commune de Belleville was annexed by Paris in 1860. The singer Edith Piaf was born on a street near here. The Parc de Belleville provides splendid views over Paris, and the market on the Boulevard de Belleville mentioned in the story by Marie Desplechin is both colourful and cosmopolitan. Change here to Line 2 and go to **Philippe Auguste**.

Philippe Auguste

The only station to be named after royalty (Philippe-Auguste reigned from 1180 to 1223), this station was the site of another tax barrier, the Barrière des Rats. It is the closest stop for the main gate of the famous Père Lachaise cemetery, where the man in Boulanger's story was attending (or trying not to attend) his aunt's funeral. The cemetery houses the remains of many famous people, among them

Oscar Wilde, Balzac, Jim Morrison, Molière, and Gérard de Nerval. The Communards fought their last battle here, among the tombs, in May 1871. They are commemorated at the Mur des Fédérés. Walk to **Père-Lachaise** metro and take Line 3 for **Opéra**.

Opéra

As in Colette's story, written in 1916, the streets around the Opéra Garnier have always been amongst the most congested in Paris, and this was even more so before the metro was built here in 1904. The original plan was to have one of Hector Guimard's famous Art Nouveau entrances, but it was decided to build a marble entrance instead, so as not to spoil the view of the Opéra itself. From **Opéra** take Line 7 to **Porte de la Villette**.

Porte de la Villette

The 'portes' or gates referred to in the names of several metro terminuses were gates in the walled defences of Paris, later demolished. The girls in Annie Saumont's story would have taken frequent trips to this station on their way to the planetarium to look at the stars. The Cité des Sciences in the Parc de la Villette, the biggest science-and-technology museum in Europe, bears no resemblance to the small Gallo-Roman village (*la villette*) that grew up along the original Roman road to Flanders. This modern complex was constructed upon the steel trusses of an abattoir sales-hall and opened in 1986. It now comprises a planetarium, cinemas (*la géode*), libraries, and aquarium and is especially popular with children and teenagers. From this metro stop take Line 7 back to the **Gare de l'Est** and change to Line 5 for **Bastille**.

Bastille

The most symbolic event in the French Revolution took place here in 1789, when the Bastille fortress, symbol of French authority, was stormed on 14 July. The statue in the centre of the square commemorates the Revolution of 1830. Balzac lived in a garret in the nearby Rue de Lesdiguières in 1819 and 1820. Near to the Place de la Bastille are the new opera-house, the Bassin de l'Arsenal (a marina), and a pleasant walk created in recent years called the Promenade Plantée. A short walk from here towards the Faubourg Saint-Antoine takes you to the Rue de Lappe and another, slightly longer, walk down the Rue de Charonne to the metro station **Charonne**.

Charonne

On 8 February 1962, at the end of the war of Algerian Independence, eight people suffocated at this metro station while taking refuge from the police who, led by their chief, Maurice Papon, were putting down a left-wing demonstration against the far-right nationalist OAS (Organisation de l'Armée Secrète). Fajardie recalls the violence at the metro in his story 'Rue des Larmes' ('Street of Tears'). From **Charonne** go to **Nation** on line 9 (or walk), change to Line 6, and go to **Glacière**.

Glacière

Historically this area, where the river Bièvre flows into the Seine, was known for its ponds and wetlands, and ice was collected here in the winter for storage and use during the summer. The name Glacière means 'ice-box'. A short walk from here is the prison where the father in Paul Fournel's story was incarcerated, and which held violent criminals, as well as members of the Resistance during the Second World War. Jacques Mesrine, well known in Britain as the subject of the films *Killer Instinct* and *Public Enemy No. 1*, was an inmate there. Return on Line 6 to **Place d'Italie** and change to Line 7. Get out at **Place Monge**.

Place Monge

Named after Gaspard Monge, a mathematician, this metro stop is the best one to get off at for the Rue Amyot where Modigliani and Jeanne Hébuterne lived, and not far from here is the Place de la Contrescarpe, the location for Martine Delerm's other story, 'There or Elsewhere'. A short walk up the Rue Mouffetard will take you to the church of Saint-Etienne behind the Panthéon, and the statue of Saint Geneviève, the subject of Jacques de Voragine's account. Now either return to **Jussieu** and take Line 10 for **Odéon**, or walk down the Rue Soufflot towards the Luxembourg gardens, at the bottom of the street.

Odéon

This is the most convenient station for the Jardin du Luxembourg. The station Luxembourg itself is only on the RER (*réseau express régional*) line. This is the jumping-off point for three stories in this collection: Martine Delerme's story about Modigliani takes place partly in the street outside the museum situated at the bottom of the Luxembourg. Maupassant's story about the two elderly people who perform the minuet is set at the other end of the gardens, in a wild part which, despite a petition being mounted, was demolished under Napoleon III. Zola's piece about the snow is also set at this end near the Observatoire. Go back to **Odéon** and take Line 4 to **Châtelet/Les Halles**.

Les Halles

Gérard de Nerval describes his wanderings through the market in 1852. But the old meat-and-vegetable market, immortalized by Zola in his series of Rougon Macquart novels as 'Le Ventre de Paris' (the belly of Paris), existed until 1971, when the market was moved to Rungis, outside the city. In the 1960s you could still go there in the small hours and eat onion soup while you watched the traders. Then the decrepit buildings were pulled down and replaced by the modern emporium of the Forum des Halles. Take the Line 4 metro from here to the **Porte de Clignancourt**.

Porte de Clignancourt

The station at the northern end of the busy Line 4 that links with **Porte d'Orléans** in the south. The hero of Andrée Chedid's story meets his old flame at the entrance to this metro. Clignancourt is the site of the famous flea-market, also known as Saint-Ouen. This district used to belong to the Abbey of Saint-Denis, which was annexed to Paris in 1860. Back to **Barbès-Rochechouart** on line 4 then change to line 2 for **Rome**.

Rome

Colette, the unfortunate wife of the composer Janoty in Banville's story, might today have taken the metro to the station called **Rome** before buying her prawns at the organic market on the Boulevard des Batignolles on a Saturday morning. This district, formerly a village outside Paris until it was annexed by Napoleon III in 1860, was the artistic centre for the Impressionist group around Manet, who lived in the Rue Médéric and who met in the years between 1869 and 1875. Formerly characterized by its multi-ethnic occupation, Batignolles has now become a fashionable place to live. There is a pleasant park in the English style, with a children's playground and duck-ponds. Four stops further along you reach **Ternes**.

Ternes

The name comes from the Latin 'villa externa', the town outside the walls, which was brought within the jurisdiction of Paris in 1860. In Simenon's story the impression one gets is of a rather louche district, but this area is now fairly upmarket. The Avenue des Ternes leads to the Bois de Boulogne and the smart seventeenth arrondissement. At the following metro, **Charles de Gaulle**, you change to Line 1 and make your way to the **Porte de Vincennes**.

Porte de Vincennes

This metro station, where the traveller in Dufresne's story gets on every day, was the original eastern terminus, until the metro line was extended to the Château de Vincennes in 1934. The château in the extensive park is famous for having held the Marquis de Sade prisoner and also for the Sèvres porcelain originally made there. Back along the same line to **Saint-Paul**.

Saint-Paul

The Jewish community lived in this area, the Marais, and many of them, like the hero of Fleischman's story, were forced to move out to escape the victimization of the Jews during the Second World War. The nearby Place des Vosges, formerly known as the Place Royale, built by Henri IV at the beginning of the seventeenth century, is the oldest and probably the most beautiful square in Paris. Back to **Châtelet** for Line 4 to **Saint-Germain**.

Saint-Germain-des-Prés

This metro is at the heart of the Left Bank, famous in the twentieth century for its artistic and intellectual life. Near here are the Café de Flore and Les Deux Magots where Sartre and Simone de Beauvoir, among other intellectuals, met and talked in the years after the Second World War. A short walk from the metro, in the direction of the river, is the Rue des Saints Pères, described by Maupassant in his story of the landlady. Walk to the nearest metro, **Sèvres-Babylone**, and take Line 12 to **Lamarck-Caulaincourt**.

Lamarck-Caulaincourt

This station entrance is flanked on either side by steps leading up to Montmartre, described by Nerval. To appreciate the view over the plain of Saint-Denis, go up to the Sacré Coeur and over the hill at the back. The station is named after two men: Caulaincourt was Foreign Minister from 1813 to 1814; Lamarck (1744–1829) was a soldier, renowned naturalist, and Professor of Zoology in the Paris Natural History Museum, who made an important contribution to the study of evolution.

Notes on the Stories

Introduction

Raymond Queneau: (1903–76), poet, novelist, founder of Oulipo (Ouvroir de littérature potentielle). Books include *Exercices de style* (1947) and *Zazie dans le métro* (1959).

Abbé Pierre: (1912–2007), Catholic priest, much-loved champion of the homeless and destitute.

RER: Réseau Express Régional, opened in 1977.

Hector Guimard: (1867–1942), architect of French Art Nouveau.

rotting bananas: John Lichfield, in an article in *The Independent*, 19 December 1998.

1.

The Gare du Nord, built in 1846, was initially too small and was demolished fourteen years later and its façade moved to Lille. Jacques Hittorff redesigned the complex between 1861 and 1864. The sculptures on the façade described by Jacques Réda represent the cities served by the company. The interior of the station was completely rebuilt in 1889 to cope with the increasing volume of traffic.

2.

The legend of Saint Julien of Mans, champion of the poor, can be found in Jacques de Voragine's account in the *Légende dorée*, written sometime towards the end of the thirteenth century.

lendit: ('l'endit' = 'announced') festival began in 1053 with a display of relics of Christ in Saint-Denis. It became a fair for merchants to sell cloth, in June, when the bishop of Paris blessed it and the members of the university arrived there to buy their parchment.

Brunetto Latini: figures in the Seventh Circle of Dante's *Inferno* in Canto 15, with sodomites, but the portrait Dante paints of him is nevertheless affectionate.

Mansart: François Mansart, architect (1598–1666), credited with introducing classicism into French architecture. The 'mansarde' (garret room) is named after him.

3.

La Belle Vie: the sign reads, ironically for the heroine, '*Beautiful Life*'.

Doliprane…Lysanxia: types of painkiller available in France.

Spasfon: a medicine used for digestive troubles.

Monoprix: the popular French department store.

5.

A Little Accident: Colette's story, written in 1916, reflects the tense atmosphere in Paris during the First World War when nationalistic feelings were running high.

6.

Fang-Citron: presumably an advert for a lemon drink.

Paris-Turf: equivalent of the *Racing Post* in the UK.

7.

Rue de Lesdiguières: Balzac lived here between 1819 and 1820, at the beginning of his career.

Monsieur: title of the brother of a reigning monarch, here Charles X, brother of Louis XVIII.

Ambigu-Comique: a theatre known for putting on vaudeville and light comedy.

la Courtille: part of Belleville, known for the celebrations and feastings in its cafés at carnival time.

Quinze-Vingts: an institution for the blind going back to medieval times.

Père Canard: a play on words: a 'canard' is a false note; and he is called Cane.

Livre d'Or: the directory of nobles in the Republic of Venice.

Casa d'Oro: the fifteenth-century palace in Venice faced with gold.

provveditore: the position as local governor frequently held by a noble at some point in his life.

in the wells: the wells or 'pozzi' were eighteen cells on the ground floor of the Doge's palace in Venice. The 'piombi' were the rooms where nobles were often held, under the roof.

the Ten: the council of ten ministers.

Madame du Barry: favourite of Louis XV.

Gil Blas: hero of the eighteenth-century picaresque novel of that name by Lesage.

Bicêtre: a famous mental hospital outside Paris.

destroyed by Napoleon: the Republic of Venice lost its independence to Napoleon when he conquered it in 1797.

Super flumina Babylonis: 'By the rivers of Babylon', opening of Psalm 137, a lament of the exiled Hebrews.

8.

Rue des Larmes: Fajardie's story about the Rue de Lappe is called 'Street of Tears'.

Jean Ferrat: (1930–2010), a left-wing chansonnier, as was *Francis Lemarque* (1917–2002), who was born in the Rue de Lappe. *Maurice Chevalier* (1888–1972) was criticized for his perceived collaboration with the Nazis.

Salaisons d'Auvergne: (lit: salt products), the Auvergne region in France is noted for its cold meats and pork products.

Louis-Ferdinand Céline: (1894–1961), doctor and author of *Voyage au bout de la nuit*, wrote a thesis on Semmelweiss in 1924.

Balajo: a club in the Rue de Lappe.

'*Inno*': a chain of shops in both France and Belgium.

Pierre Overney: the militant killed in 1972 by a security guard at Renault when he tried to commemorate the massacre of 1962 by inciting the workers at the factory to violence.

UJCML: Union des Jeunesses Communistes Marxistes-Léninistes, a Communist youth movement.

9.

La Santé prison: the boy's father serves his term in this famous prison. The guillotine was last used there in 1972.

11.

Attila the Hun: threatened to attack Paris in 451 but was prevented, according to legend, by Saint Genevieve's prayers.

Vincent de Beauvais: *c.*1190–1264, wrote the *Speculum maius* ('Great Mirror'), a medieval compendium of knowledge.

Childeric: 440–81, king of the Franks.

Simon the Stylite: the ascetic Christian saint who spent thirty-seven years living on a small platform at the top of a pillar.

sacred fire: erisypelas, a disease also known as holy fire or St Anthony's fire.

12.

Colarossi: the art school in Paris attended by Jeanne Hébuterne.

Zborowski: the Polish friend of Modigliani who supported him financially and set up exhibitions for him.

13.

nursery gardens: a third of the original gardens disappeared in 1865 by imperial decree, including the wild gardens, changing the nature of the Luxembourg for ever.

culotte à pont: trousers worn in the Ancien Régime, with a panel that buttoned at the front rather like German 'lederhosen'.

King Louis XV: French king, 1715–74.

14.

Observatoire: the Observatory in Paris was founded in 1667 and is the largest national research centre for astronomy and astrophysics.

15.

These are five sections from *Les Nuits d'Octobre*, published October and November 1852 in *L'Illustration*.

Vignola: Giacomo da Vignola (1507–73); his *Rule of the Five Orders of Architecture* (1562) remained a standard textbook for three centuries. Nerval, like many people, disapproved of the neoclassical additions and alterations to Saint Eustache.

Raspail: François-Vincent Raspail (1794–1878); medical scientist and republican politician, he did much for public health.

Domfront, 'unhappy town': '*Ah! Domfront! Ville de malheur! / Arrivé à midi, pendu à une heure!*' ('Domfront, unhappy town / Arrived at noon, hanged at one'). Said to be the last words of a man hanged there in 1574 during the Wars of Religion.

blanquette of Limoux: first mentioned in 1531, is considered to be France's oldest sparkling white wine.

contango: 'The percentage which a buyer of stock pays to the seller to postpone transfer to the next or any future settling day' (*OED*).

games of chance: gambling was banned in France on 31 December 1837.

a red mouse: Goethe, *Faust, Part I*, ll. 4178–9.

Vadé: Jean-Joseph Vadé (1720–57), author of humorous verse, parodies, light comedies in which he made free use of the coarse jargon of the fish-market.

the 'Strong Men': ('les forts'), a guild of well-qualified and highly specialized porters in Les Halles.

Robbé: Pierre-Honoré Robbé de Beauveset (1714–92), author of obscene and anticlerical verses.

Jean Goujon: (*c*.1510–*c*.1566), French Renaissance sculptor and architect. He collaborated with the architect Pierre Lescaut (*c*.1510–78) on the Fontaine des Innocents, now in the Square des Innocents.

Golden Nobles...: a very free translation of 'Pommes de reinette et pomm's d'apis', a popular market song of around 1800.

Silenus: a drunken satyr. Bacchantes were wild female followers of Dionysus, god of wine; they tore Orpheus to pieces.

cornets and marmots: kinds of headdress for women.

estimable dockers: 'les portefaix', a highly organized dockers' cooperative in Marseilles, managing the work and investing in the business.

verjus: a drink or culinary ingredient made from the juice of green grapes or other unripe fruits.

Barras: Paul, vicomte de Barras (1755–1829), politician especially powerful in the Directory (1795–9), famous for luxury and self-indulgence.

merveilleuses … Mirliflores: extravagantly fashionable socialites, female and male, under the Directory.

Strasburg station: now the Gare de l'Est, opened 1850. Nerval continued his wanderings by train from there, as far as Meaux.

17.

Folies-Marigny: this theatre in the eighth arrondissement, set up in the nineteenth century, still exists.

Heinrich Heine: German Romantic poet, he left Germany in 1831 and lived in Paris until his death in 1856.

Sganarelle: character in Moliere's play of that name. Sganarelle was a 'cocu imaginaire', i.e. he imagined wrongly that his wife was unfaithful.

Figaro: see Act 3 of *Le Mariage de Figaro* by Beaumarchais, where Figaro is trying to find out who his parents are.

Café Anglais … Maison d'Or: two famous contemporary restaurants in Paris.

Maître Cornelius: a short novel by Balzac about a married woman whose lover apprentices himself to a silversmith called Maître Cornelius.

Judic... Granier... Mme Théo: Anna Judic, Jeanne Granier, and Mme Théo were famous Parisian actresses; the first is said to have been the inspiration for Zola's character Nana.

Carabosse: the wicked fairy in Perrault's *The Sleeping Beauty*.

Mon frère pompe...: frivolous song about a fireman, with suggestive words.

La Patti: famous opera singer, 1843–1919.

Funambules: the theatre where shows of physical dexterity containing many transformation scenes, like pantomimes, were performed.

J'ai du bon tabac...: French nursery rhymes with correspondingly simple tunes.

Brocken: the highest peak in the Harz mountains, famed for its Witches Sabbath, important in Goethe's *Faust*.

Cinna: see the last act of that play (by Corneille). Cinna plotted against Augustus but was pardoned by him.

18.

complet: fully booked.

Quai de l'Horloge: the police station on the Île de la Cité, so called because of its proximity to the 'horloge' (clock) on the Palais de Justice.

20.

'Sortez de là, vous!': 'Get out of here!' The neighbour obviously thinks Klergz is drunk. The polite form of address in French would never be used for an animal.

22.

Nerval returned from Germany at the end of July 1854 and soon went back into Dr Blanche's clinic in Passy (the 'villa out of town'). But he got himself discharged from there on 19 October and his life between then and his suicide three months later was wandering and desperate. *Promenades et souvenirs*, which in lucid prose describes his looking for somewhere to live, was published in three instalments in *L'Illustration*, 30 December 1854, and 6 January and 3 February 1855. He was dead when the last one came out.

Place du Louvre: Nerval lived at 4 rue Saint-Thomas-du-Louvre between 1848 and 1850. He was evicted to allow the extension of the Rue de Rivoli. He was at 9 Rue du Mail in March and April 1850.

Fénelon: from Book I of his *Télémaque* (1699).

Grétry... chanterelle: A.-E.-M. Grétry (1741–1813) was a composer. A *chanterelle* is a singing-bird used as a decoy to trap other birds.

a good deal in Montmartre: Nerval spent several months of 1841 in Dr Blanche's first clinic, la Folie-Sandrin, in the Rue Norvins, Montmartre.

having been virtuous: phrase borrowed (and altered) from the seventeenth-century letter-writer Mme de Sévigné.

Cuvier: Baron Georges Léopold Chrétien Frédéric Dagobert Cuvier (1769–1832) was a French zoologist and statesman, who established the sciences of comparative anatomy and paleontology. In his *Description géologique des environs de Paris* there is a chapter on the fossils of Montmartre.

Rue de l'Empereur: now the Rue Lepic.

Butte des Moulins: an artificial mound made during work on fortifications in 1536. It had windmills on top and was situated at the junction of the Rue des Petits-Champs and the Rue Sainte-Anne (Ier arrondissement).

You will even find a vineyard here, the last: this seems not to be the one (on the Rue de la Vigne) which survives today, but another, close to the Château des Brouillards (where Nerval lived for a while in May 1846).

a second Bacchus: writers such as François Dupuis and Alexandre Lenoir, in the spirit of the *philosophes*, readily assimilated Christianity into the ancient religions of Egypt, Greece, and Rome.

the watering-place: formerly in the cobbled depression outside 15 Rue de l'Abreuvoir. This street runs along the back wall of la Folie-Sandrin, Dr Blanche's clinic.

Werther: by Goethe, published 1774. Nerval was a passionate admirer of Goethe and translated Part I of his *Faust*.

the Chemin des Boeufs: for part of its length it runs along the present Rue Marcadet.

Monsieur Vautour: a character in a one-act vaudeville of 1805.

Laviron: Gabriel Laviron, a painter, born 1806, died 1849 fighting for Garibaldi at the siege of Rome.

Notes on the Authors

Jacques Réda, born 1929, has written many stories and essays set in Paris. This is one of his studies of railway stations and is taken from *Châteaux des courants d'air*.

Julien Green, 1900–98; his parents were American but he was born and brought up in Paris. During the Second World War, from the Occupation to the Liberation, he lived in the United States.

Marie Desplechin, born 1959, is a journalist and writer. She has published several collections of short stories, including *Trop sensibles*, and a best-selling novel, *Sans moi*.

Daniel Boulanger, born 1922, is a prolific writer of short stories, especially renowned for his sketches of provincial life. This story about the cemetery is among the few set in Paris.

Colette (Sidonie-Gabrielle Colette), 1873–1954, born in a little village in Burgundy, moved to Paris when she married and wrote frequent sketches of Parisian life. A prolific writer all her life, she died in an apartment overlooking the Palais-Royal gardens.

Annie Saumont, born 1927, the 'grande dame' of the modern short story in French has influenced many younger writers. She is known for her breathless, stream-of-consciousness style.

Honoré de Balzac, 1799–1850, is known mainly for his achievement as a novelist, but at one time was known as the 'roi de la nouvelle' (king of the short story) and regarded primarily as a writer of stories, which were collected in his great work *La Comédie humaine*.

Frédéric Fajardie, 1947–2008, left-wing writer and political activist, was one of the most prolific writers of short stories in recent times.

Paul Fournel, born 1947, writer, poet, and president of Oulipo, whose founder member was Raymond Queneau, has served as cultural attaché at the French Embassy in London.

Martine Delerm, born 1950, is a writer and illustrator who has written numerous stories. She is married to the writer Philippe Delerm and is the mother of the singer Vincent Delerm.

Jacques de Voragine (*c.*1228–98) was a Genoese priest and is mainly famous as the author of the *Légende dorée* ('The Golden Legend'), a Latin collection of the lives of the saints.

Guy de Maupassant, 1850–93, possibly France's greatest short-story writer. Maupassant was from Normandy but spent a good deal of his life in Paris, and wrote many humorous as well as touching stories about the society he found there.

Émile Zola, 1840–1902, was born and died in Paris. He is chiefly known for his series of novels *Les Rougon-Macquart*, many of which deal with aspects of Paris, for instance *Le Ventre de Paris* about Les Halles market or *Au bonheur des dames* about the rise of a department store; but between 1864 and 1874 he also wrote many fine short stories and texts like the one translated here, 'Snow'.

Gérard de Nerval (Gérard Labrunie), 1808–55, one of the great French Romantic poets, translator of Goethe and Heine and friend of Gautier, suffered badly from a mental disorder in his short life, and hanged himself in the Rue de la Vieille Lanterne, which was demolished in 1855.

Andrée Chedid was born in Cairo in 1920 and has lived in Paris since 1946. She is widely known for her poetry as well as her stories.

Théodore de Banville, 1823–91, poet, writer, dramatist, and theatre critic, spent most of his life in Paris. Among his works are many stories and anecdotes noting the foibles of his fellow Parisians, such as this one, 'The Cab'.

Georges Simenon, 1903–89, is a Belgian writer of nearly 200 novels and short stories. The chief character of many of them is the detective, Inspector Maigret.

Claude Dufresne, 1920–2005, writer and broadcaster in radio and television, is one of the contributors to a collection of stories from *Le Temps de vivre*, Jacques Pradel's famous programme on the French radio station France-Inter, which ran for many years.

Cyrille Fleischman, a Jewish writer born in Paris in 1941, writes principally about the Marais area, where many Jewish families lived.

Selected Further Reading

On Paris

Paris, Guides Bleus, Harrap (1991), a comprehensive guide to Paris, with a wealth of useful background information, detailed history, and maps.

Paris par arrondissement, Éditions L'Indispensable (1988), a useful pocket guide for getting around the capital.

Paris: The Secret History, by Andrew Hussey (Viking, 2006).

Dictionnaire Historique des Rues de Paris (2 volumes), ed. Jacques Hillairet, (Les Editions de Minuit 1997). These two volumes contain detailed histories of each street and the buildings in them as well as photographs of streets in Paris in different decades.

Eugène Atget's Paris, by Andreas Krase, ed. Hans Christian Adam (Taschen, 2001). Photographic evidence of what Paris looked like in the first two decades of the twentieth century.

The Streets of Paris, by Richard Cobb, with photographs by Nicholas Breach (Duckworth, 1980). What Paris looked like in the last two decades of the twentieth century.

The Time Out Book of Paris Walks, ed. Andrew White (Penguin, 1999).

Two books on the evolution of Paris from Roman times to the present, both extremely well-written and entertaining:

Seven Ages of Paris, Portrait of a City, by Alistair Horne (Macmillan, 2002).

Paris, Biography of a City, by Colin Jones (Penguin, 2004).

On the Metro

Metro Stop Paris, History from the City's Heart, by Gregor Dallas (John Murray, 2008).

Paris by Metro, An Underground History, by Arnold Delaney (Interlink Publishing Group, 2006).

Paris Metro Handbook, by Brian Hardy (Capital Transport, 1999).

Notre métro, by Jean Robert (Omnes et Cie, Paris, 1967).

Le guide des stations de métro and *Au fil des lignes du métro*:
These two booklets are often sold by itinerants in the metro for a couple of euros.

Anthologies of French short stories

The Oxford Book of French Short Stories, ed. Elizabeth Fallaize (OUP, 2002).

The Time Out Book of Paris Short Stories, ed. Nicholas Royle (Penguin, 1999). These are mainly by Anglophone writers.

XciTés, ed. Georgia de Chamberet (Flamingo, 1999). A selection of stories and extracts from novels by twentieth-century French writers in the 1980s and 1990s.

French Short Stories, vols 1 and 2, eds. Pamela Lyon and Simon Lee (Penguin, 1966 and 1972).

Short Stories in French, New Penguin Parallel Text, trans. and ed. Richard Coward (Penguin, 1999). These are bilingual texts and therefore useful for language students.

On the short story

The Short Story, by Ian Reid, in *The Critical Idiom*, ed. John T. Jump (Methuen, 1977).

La Nouvelle française contemporaine, by Annie Mignard (Ministère des Affaires Étrangères, 2000). This is in three languages and has a helpful list of short-story writers.

Publisher's Acknowledgements

1. 'Gare du Nord', by Jacques Réda, from *Châteaux des courants d'air*, Gallimard, 1986.
2. 'Saint-Julien-le-Pauvre', by Julien Green, from *Paris*, Éditions du Champvallon, 1983.
3. 'Pluie d'été', by Marie Desplechin, from *Un pas de plus*, Éditions Page à page, 2005.
4. 'Délicatesse', by Daniel Boulanger, from *Les Noces du Merle*, Éditions de la Table Ronde, 1963.
5. 'Le Petit Accident', by Colette, Bibliothèque de la Pléiade, Gallimard, 1986.
6. 'Si c'était un dimanche', by Annie Saumont (by kind permission of the author).
7. 'Facino Cane', by Honoré de Balzac, from *Balzac Short Stories*, ed. by A.W. Raitt, OUP, 1964.
8. 'Rue des Larmes', by Frédéric Fajardie, from *Nouvelles d'un siècle l'autre*, Éditions Fayard, 2006.
9. 'Roman', by Paul Fournel (by kind permission of the author).
10. 'Là ou ailleurs', by Martine Delerm, from *Décalages*, Éditions Fayard, 2008.
11. 'Sainte Geneviève', by Jacques de Voragine, from *La Légende dorée*, Éditions Rombaldi, 1942.
12. 'Expomodigliani.com', by Martine Delerm, from *Décalages*, Éditions Fayard, 2008.

13. 'Minuet', by Guy de Maupassant, Bibliothèque de la Pléiade, Gallimard 1974.
14. 'La Neige', by Émile Zola, from *Contes et nouvelles* 1, Flammarion, 2008.
15. 'La Halle', by Gérard de Nerval, from *Les Nuits d'Octobre*, Bibliothèque de la Pléiade, Gallimard, 1993.
16. 'Face au présent', by Andrée Chedid, from *À la mort, à la vie*, Flammarion, 1992.
17. 'Le Fiacre', by Théodore de Banville from *Le Génie des Parisiennes*, Éditions Mille et Une Nuits, 2002.
18. 'Le Petit Restaurant à Ternes', by Georges Simenon, Presses de la Cité, 1974.
19. 'Romance métropolitaine', by Claude Dufresne, from *Contes à rebours, histoires et nouvelles du temps de vivre*, Éditions Mengès, 1976.
20. 'Le Voisin de la Rue de Jarente', by Cyrille Fleischman, from *Retour au métro Saint-Paul*, Librio, 2001.
21. 'La Patronne', by Guy de Maupassant, Bibliothèque de la Pléiade, Gallimard, 1996.
22. 'La Butte Montmartre', by Gérard de Nerval, from *Promenades et souvenirs*, Bibliothèque de la Pléiade, Gallimard, 1993.

Map

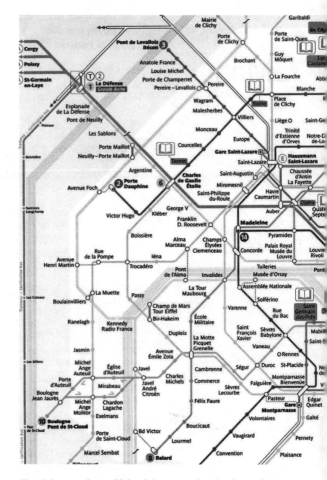

Key: Metro stations with book icon are related to the stories

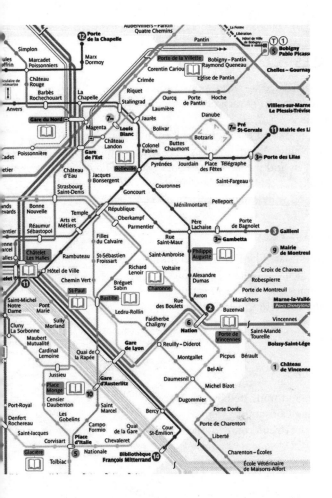

Also published by Oxford University Press

PARIS TALES

Chosen and translated by Helen Constantine
Stories old and new, from each of the capital's arrondissements
and quartiers
'Would-be flâneurs and Paris lovers will enjoy Helen Constan-
tine's collection. What emerges ... is a powerful affinity
between Paris and the fantastic.' *Times Literary Supplement*
'A smartly mixed cocktail of 22 Parisian tales.' *The Independent*
'An excellent and wide-ranging collection.' *The Times*

FRENCH TALES

Chosen and translated by Helen Constantine
A story from each of France's 22 regions.
'Immensely enjoyable.' *France Magazine*
'An intriguing collection.' *The Times*
'The tales have been translated elegantly.' *Times Literary
Supplement*

BERLIN TALES

Stories chosen and translated by Lyn Marven
Edited by Helen Constantine
Evocative stories from contemporary and twentieth-century
Berlin